FIGHT, KID!

MICHAEL JOHNSTON

ISBN 978-1-7346177-0-2

Printed in the United States of America

First Edition

Book design by Xavier Comas

For more information please contact:
michaeljohnstonbooks@gmail.com

Everyone has a plan 'till they get punched in the mouth.
—Mike Tyson

1

———————

Benny Schultz was an ex-professional boxer who had held a record of 12-1 but retired and opened a gym in his hometown of Jersey City. He trained young men who had big ideas of big wins, but Benny knew the truth. He knew the taste of big defeat. He knew what it was like to feel the canvas and not want to get back up. Skipping rope and hitting bags, these kids—they were all kids in his eyes—couldn't even begin to understand what real boxing was all about. Didn't matter the race, the size, the weight, the family—if there had been a kid who really wanted to be a fighter, then Benny had never met one. Not in his gym. But then he met nineteen-year-old Keith Way. And Keith Way could punch. But he wasn't tall. He was five-foot-ten. And he didn't weigh enough, only 177 pounds. He was a small cruiserweight—a small cruiserweight who would rise through the amateur ranks and build his own professional record of 12-0 with Benny as his trainer. But Keith Way wanted to be the heavyweight champion of the world. Too bad he was white and too bad he wasn't Irish.

The trainer and his fighter sat across from each other at Benny's favorite restaurant, the Empress Diner. The humid summer air was no good for a boxer or for an old man with too little to lose.

"Eat!" he screamed.

"I am eating," the fighter said.

"Eat more!"

Keith had eaten mostly beans, pancakes, and chocolate cake with chocolate frosting for the last eighteen days. In the first five days of training camp, he had a strength trainer and nutritionist with him. His nutritionist quit on the sixth day. His strength trainer followed soon after. Yet after two weeks of carbohydrates and constipation, Keith Way, a cruiserweight contender who wanted to move up weight classes, still could not tip the scales in his favor. Angry that his stomach couldn't handle another ounce of garlic bread or deep-fried Oreo, angrier was his trainer that Keith couldn't eat more. It made Benny weep thinking about the potential this boy could have at cruiserweight if he took a couple more fights. Won a belt. Played the game. Nothing crazy. Nothing over-the-top. More muscle. That's what he was gonna need. More muscle.

"Listen, kid. They pitted us up against a bruiser of a motherfucker."

The scar under Benny's left eye twitched. Whenever he looked in the mirror, it helped remind him about the ways of this life. Big ol' boy from Atlantic City. Took him down in the late rounds. Never saw it coming. A flash of brilliant light, stars of blue and gray. The headache lasted weeks. Doctor said concussion. The scar permanent in the way the moon brings the night, the way the sun brings the day, the way sweat had once made him feel; this tale was as old as the sea. Felt older than him.

The only part of him that wasn't scarred in fact was his hands: the same color as the white wraps he wrapped around them a thousand times before, the cotton odor a permanent perfume he dreamed about instead of the women he had stopped dreaming about. These memories seemed rushed. Seemed fake. Seemed far away.

"You've only had three pancakes. Put more butter on them. And syrup. Syrup is good for your tits."

Keith Way, 12-0 cruiserweight contender and heavyweight pretender, couldn't even think about another bite. "Coach, I'm gonna puke . . ."

"If you puke, you're eating it again!" Benny yelled. *I taught him all he knows; he's going to doubt me now?* he thought.

"I can eat more in a couple of hours. Seriously, my stomach's gonna explode. And if that happens, then . . . no fight, right?"

"You're an idiot," Benny said. "Fine. You don't want

to eat? Then don't eat. But if you come in underweight, well . . . Good luck trying to get another fight with Buster Davis."

"Buster Davis is just that, a buster," Keith joked.

"Yeah? Well, he's a buster with bigger tits than you!"

"What's your obsession with men's tits?" Keith asked. "Why don't you ever call them pecs?"

"My obsession with tits?!" Benny screamed. "Tits are life, kid. Nurtured you into life. Tits on a woman. Nothing better. Tits on a well-built, muscular boxer? Well, that's better than tits on a woman. Yep, I said it."

"Can we just put this stuff in a box, and I'll eat it at the gym later? I really don't feel well."

"It's your career, kid," he said. "And mine."

The trainer and his fighter left the Empress Diner. Aromatic scents swept from the eatery and into the parking lot—not uncommon this time of year— mixing with the summer fragrances of New Jersey. Benny welcomed them; he liked the way the corned beef smelled on the plates in passing waiters' arms, how the French toast curdled with abnormally hot butter—smelled so good it made the diner's usually dirty glasses look almost clean.

They got into Benny's Cadillac. Benny always liked Cadillacs because it was the car he thought he would never own, and now he owned one. But now he was old, and so was the car, and so was his desire to own one. Keith never said anything about the ripped interior, or the turn signals that didn't work, or the missing brake light, or the way his trainer grimaced when driving it over potholes. *Poor thing,* Keith thought. Not about Benny, but the car. Then there was the price of gas. The Cadillac ate it up like candy. No one at the gym said anything about the Cadillac's awful paint job either. Or the two missing hubcaps. Why say anything? *Let the old man enjoy it,* they all thought. Other trainers at different gyms, in bigger cities, drove new SUVs like Escalades, Suburbans, and G-Wagens. But other trainers also had other fighters who made lots of money. And Keith Way did not make a lot of money. And Keith Way blamed this on having only 11,026 followers on Instagram as of eight seconds ago, when he last checked his notifications.

He needs to eat more, Benny thought. And he was right.

"I'm going to put this in the fridge for later," Keith said.

Benny took his glasses off and cleaned them with a handkerchief Keith had never seen not dirty. "I don't think the fridge is gonna be big enough for all that food you didn't eat," Benny joked.

"How many rounds of sparring do you want to do today? My wrist is still kinda bothering me. Maybe we can take it easy. Increase the cardio."

"No. We're sparring ten rounds today. I already have Anthony Maliganoni coming in from Philly to work with you. No, we're sparring today. And if you'd eat more, your wrist wouldn't hurt."

"You think Anthony still fights like he did when I beat him two years ago? Remember that, Coach? That was my third pro fight. Got him with the left to the liver. Dude went down hard."

"I remember, kid. That was a great punch. That was also at light heavyweight. I wish you'd eat more."

"He also has a six-inch reach on me. Longer than Buster's. But Buster Davis ain't reaching for success like I am."

Benny could puke. "Yeah, kid. Reaching for success. He's also reaching to knock your skinny ass the fuck out. You see the tits on him? Hasn't taken a fight past the fifth round. Brutal power with that right hand, kid. Brutal power."

"He ain't gonna knock me out. No way! Not with this head movement, and speed, and focus, and heart. Come on, Coach! Weight is just a number on a scale, not the measurement of your determination."

"*Determination*, kid?" Benny said with the enthusiasm of a grape. "That's what wins fights. *Determination* . . . Get your head out of your ass, will ya? Hitting and not being hit is what wins fights, kid. Being determined to not get hit, that's what boxing is. Didn't you learn anything from Floyd?"

"Well, yeah, of course. Not getting hit helps. But so does determination. And a good left hook. Always need a good left hook."

Benny stared at his boxer with sad, dry eyelids. "I got hit a lot, kid. I don't want you to get hit that way. Especially at heavyweight. These are strong boys. Strong boys. You need to be ready for them. Ready for their power. Ready for what they are going to bring to you."

"Will you stop with the lecturing please? I know what this is. Sabrina won't shut up about it. How can I not know?"

"You two still dating?"

"How about four rounds of sparring?"

"We're going ten, and don't ask me again," Benny said. The trainer held high hopes that the rounds would knock a little sense into his fighter. Knock into him that leaving the cruiserweight division was not the right course of action. Not yet. "We paid good money to get Anthony to agree to this. And that drive from Philly? Awful."

"Six," Keith said.

"Ten or I quit now."

"You're not gonna quit." Keith laughed. "And fine, we'll do eight."

"Enough!"

Benny took a bit of satisfaction in winning the only kind of fight he could still win these days. Verbal fights. Fights with words. More hurtful than an unsuspecting jab. He couldn't help but miss the ring and the ropes. Wish he could still fight with his hands, because his words weren't strong enough.

"Today is going to be a good day. Good work makes for good days. Let's do good work," he said.

"I always do good work, Coach."

"You better do good work with such little food in your stomach. Seen corpses eat more than you."

"I'm gonna put in some solid rounds with Anthony," Keith said. "Relax, Coach. Ease into it. You know how I like to do it."

"If you knock him down, I'm gonna be happy. I want you to hit that motherfucker hard. Show him how we do it here in Jersey. Philly cheesesteak punk. You should be eating a Philly cheesesteak right now. With fries."

"I'm gonna focus on the jab today. First couple of rounds. Lead him into me, take away his reach, always a good approach. But if I can get him to come in close: hook, jab, jab, *boom* . . . On the ground."

"You think he's that shitty of a boxer? What's wrong with you, kid?"

"It's not that he's shitty. It's just that, well . . . I got this. Easy work."

"Funny," Benny said. "You've never fought a heavyweight fight, but you've got a heavyweight head. And that ain't a compliment. Heavyweight heads are just that, heavy."

"Who are you to talk? You fought how many amateur fights? Fifty? Sixty? How many blows to the head did you take?"

"Not enough to ignore this conversation with you."

"Hopefully not too many that you can't finish this camp. Only two weeks left."

"Two weeks? By the looks of your tits I'd say we're fucked. And not in a way that I can fuck them."

"Can we go to the gym please?" Keith asked anxiously. "I need to take a shit. Those sausage links are . . . not . . . sitting . . . pretty . . ."

Benny put the Cadillac in reverse and backed out of the diner's parking lot. He hated parking lots. Too many cars belonging to too many people whom he didn't care about. *Waste of fucking space,* he'd say if you asked him. They all were. If they weren't boxers or his wife, then they were a waste of space. Nothing worse than wasted space. The space in the back seat of his car wasted with speed bags and tape and scissors and gloves and duffel bags and granola bar wrappers and emptied water bottles and mouthpieces and an old issue of *Ring* magazine; he drove with him to the gym the same thing he drove from: disappointment. He had opened Hudson Boxing Gym to make amends to himself, to make amends to the demons in his head that he had let down along the way. The hours spent training. The burpees and push-ups and crunches and miles run. Over before it could begin. One punch. It all ended then. In New York City. Undercard. One punch.

The trainer and the fighter sat in silence the whole drive from the diner to the gym. Not because there was nothing to be said, but because there was too much to say. Not enough room in the car for all the trainer and the fighter could talk about if they had so chosen. Not enough room on this planet. By the time Hudson Boxing Gym was in front of them, it felt like they might explode from all they could have said.

The front door was stuck, rusted, something the gym's manager, Donny, still hadn't fixed. Benny cursed under his breath—*I need to fire that idiot*—as he pried it open and as Donny walked before him with a rag and bottle in hand, spraying down the heavy bags and cracking open the windows. Doing his job. What everyone in this gym should be doing. Work. Good work. Benny went to his office, kicked off his shoes, leaned back in his chair, and farted. The picture of his wife, Nesrine, was stationed in its permanent corner on his desk to keep him company when she wasn't keeping him company. *Today is going to be a good day,* he assured himself one more time. *They all need to be good days.*

"Anthony's here, Coach!" Keith yelled from around the corner.

"Tell him to start lacing his gloves up," Benny said. "And why aren't you jumping rope? Let's get going, kid."

"Anthony said he'd be down to go a couple of less rounds today too."

"The fuck did I say before? I don't care if he's lazy and twenty pounds overweight. He shouldn't be eating so much. You should!"

"I'm gonna start wrapping my hands."

"I'm gonna wrap my hands around your throat, you keep annoying me."

The trainer and the fighter went through this same routine every day. Down to the minute. But the need to reenact it each morning was essential, because routine was essential in boxing. That's what Benny preached to anybody he could get to listen him. *Routine, routine, routine.* And today would be no different.

"Mr. Maliganoni, thank you for gracing us with your presence this morning," Benny said. "Looking fit as always."

Anthony Maliganoni stood five-foot-nine and, when in shape, weighed 178 pounds. Today he weighed closer to 200 pounds. "You're still alive? Thought they'd throw you out with the rest of the garbage you got clunking up this place you call a gym."

"Anthony." Keith approached. "Meant to ask how your daughter is. Remember your dog died last time we saw each other?"

"Will you two queers stop making out and get your gloves on?" Benny pleaded. "We got work to do, kid!"

A few minutes later, Keith yelled from inside the ring across the blaring hip-hop and men grunting and girls filming themselves squatting in front of the mirror to post on Instagram. "Donny? Can you put on some Metallica?"

The sparring was hard. Exactly how Benny liked it. Exactly how it should be done. Good, hard work.

"And when he dips his head left, I want you to *shoot*

with that seven. Shoot that upper!" Benny explained between rounds in the corner, forgetting that this was sparring and not a real fight. Forgetting that not every-thing was a fight.

"It's not the weight that's got me," Keith said, gassed. "I can't see his jab coming. He keeps his hand low. He never did that before. This is good. This I need to know."

His arms rested on the top rope, the sparring not hard enough that he needed to sit on a stool. *There are no stools in sparring,* Benny would say.

"Youse homos ready over there?" Anthony asked from his corner across the ring. The sweat from his gut puddled at his feet. Better than blood. Easier to clean up.

"I'd bite that tongue, Anthony," Keith responded.

"Fuck him up," Benny demanded.

The sparring brought about a bloody nose for Anthony and a bloody ring for the gym. It would take Donny hours to scrub it out.

"Great work," Keith said, as sweat continued to vacate his pores ten minutes after their session.

"You really want to go up to heavyweight?" Anthony asked as the three men sat around on stools in the ring. "I mean, you got power, Keith. But you're pretty light."

"He won't eat!" Benny roared. "Look at his tits!"

"I don't know what's wrong with you guys, obsessed

with my weight. Big deal if I'm on the lighter side. Didn't hurt Holyfield."

"You see the traps on Holyfield?!" Benny argued. "What's wrong with you, kid? I told you this was a mistake. Big mistake. I'm the king of 'em. Look at me."

"Yeah, Keith. Cruiserweight is where you belong."

Anthony agreeing with him annoyed Benny. "Yeah, what he said that I said."

"Yeah, okay. Holyfield had great traps. And Ali could jive. And Tyson could hit," Keith protested. "But that's not what wins championships."

"It did for them," Benny said.

"Do youse guys ever not bitch at each other?" Anthony asked. "Every time I'm in this stink pit, youse guys are bitching about something new. No wonder no work gets done in here."

"Nothing but work gets done in here!" Benny roared. "Get out of my gym, you punk. Mutt of a boxer, you ask me."

"Love you too," Anthony said. "Good luck with the weight, Keith. I'll see you at the fight."

"Thanks, Anthony. Thanks for the good work today."

When Benny got home that night, Nesrine had pork chops waiting on the dinner table. He could smell them from the elevator. He didn't particularly like pork chops, or pork for that matter, but he liked that Nesrine still liked to cook for him, still liked to care for him. The people at the gym cared for him, but in that way you care for a houseplant: enough love and water to keep it alive until it dies and then you throw it out and get a new one. People could always find a new gym. They could always find something new if they wanted. But most people didn't. And Benny had always relied on this laziness in others.

The night cool and the meat warm, he retired to bed earlier than usual. The sparring session had been good, but he was worried about Keith's weight. *Why the fuck is he reaching?* he thought, as his body, which had once been young like a fighter's but now was old like a trainer's, tossed and turned. *Why can't he listen to me? He's not a natural heavyweight. And he ain't Roy Jones Jr. He could have a chance at something.*

Nesrine disrupted the thoughts she knew her husband was fighting when she climbed into bed next to him. She liked to be close to him, feel the stubble of his close-cropped beard. The scraping made her feel alive. She made him feel alive.

At the Empress Diner the next morning, Keith looked the same as the day before. Looked as if he'd lost weight even. *What an awful idea.*

"Did I ever tell you the story about my last fight?" Benny asked.

The forkful of ham and cheese omelet appeared comical as it entered Keith's mouth. "You've told me a hundred times," he said. "But if it makes you feel better..."

Benny smiled. He smiled because he could remember. He could remember the crowd and the sounds and the lights. He could remember the smells and the mouthpiece and the referee. He could remember the loss and the tears and the failure. He could remember the failure most of all.

"Great fight, kid. Should have been there. Had him all the way till the ninth. Caught me. Couldn't even tell you what punch. My legs gave out before my heart."

"It's the game," Keith said. "What we signed up for."

"Yeah, kid. *The game.*"

"Come on, don't get all mopey now. You're the one who brought it up!"

"I'm not mopey. Let's go do work."

Benny paid the bill, got up, and went out to the Cadillac, parked in its regular spot—farthest corner of the parking lot—same every time. He liked to walk a little before and after a meal. Nesrine said it was good for his heart.

"Can I show you this clip real quick?" the fighter asked his trainer after he buckled himself in.

Irritated that Keith's iPhone was always in his hand, Benny growled, "Clip? Clip of what?"

"This video Buster Davis just posted on his Instagram."

Benny hated technology, hated the change it brought. Change was no good. Fuck all those bumper stickers and feel-good mantras, change was bad in

Benny's mind. Repetition was good. Repetition and hard work. Not change.

"Why are you always on that fucking thing?"

"I'm not."

"You're on it right now!"

"I'm on it," Keith said, "because I want to show you a video."

"A video of what?" Benny asked. "What could I possibly want to watch a video of?"

"Of Buster Davis working out."

"Let me see that thing." Benny adjusted his glasses. He wore glasses because a doctor told him to, not because he needed them. Now he needed them for everything. "He looks good. Moving good. Great tits."

"This video has sixteen thousand views and 3,730 likes and he posted it two hours ago."

"Is that good?"

"Yeah, Coach. That's insane. And that's why I need to fight him."

"You need to fight him because he put a video on the internet?"

"I need to fight him," the fighter told his trainer, "because when I beat him, then I'm gonna get at least twenty thousand more followers."

"What the fuck is wrong with you kids?" Benny asked. "Is this really what the fight game has come down to?"

Keith didn't answer because he didn't know the answer. He knew that social media was the key to getting bigger fights, but that's not what Benny wanted to hear. *Benny's old,* he thought. Keith knew that if you had a big social media following, then a big-time agent would want to work with you, and Keith's agent was not a big-time agent. Keith also only had 11,192 followers on Instagram when he last checked thirty-two seconds ago. He didn't use Twitter because he wasn't witty enough. His mom had always taught him to say nothing if he had nothing to say, and Twitter was for people who had nothing to say. And pictures spoke to him more than words ever did. A good thing for a professional boxer.

"I'm worried, kid," Benny said.

"Will you please stop?" Keith asked. "It's bad for your heart."

"Buster Davis walks around 220 pounds." Benny talked fast. He talked fast when he was worried.

"All I do is eat! Let's increase the weight on strength and conditioning, put some more muscle on me."

"Buster Davis. Built like a shit brickhouse."

"Yeah. But all that bulk? Slows a man down. His fights show that."

"You think bulk is gonna slow him down? What's wrong with you, kid? Bulk is power, and power's gonna knock your ass out if you keep spending all your time on that phone. Don't care how many people like your dumb photos."

"Knock me out? Thanks for the motivation, Coach. Knock me out, pfft . . ."

"I remember when I saw Lennox Lewis. Biggest motherfucker I'd ever seen with my own eyes. Swear he was the size of a building. Genetics, kid. Can't buy genetics."

"Never knew he was British till a couple of years ago. Just like that dude from *The Wire*," Keith said. "Heard him in a post-fight interview."

"What's *The Wire*?" Benny asked. "Is that one of those videos on your Insta-whatever-the-fuck?"

"*The Wire* was a television show on HBO. Almost as good as *The Sopranos*. And it's called Instagram."

"When I was training for a fight, I was eating whole chickens with potatoes and reading Philip Roth. Made a man out of me. These phones today. You kids are fucked."

"Yeah, Coach. That's it. Fucked."

"Want to talk about a television show? Or do you want to get to the gym and talk about this fight, kid?"

"Dumb question, Coach," Keith replied with humor.

Benny wasn't in the mood for humor. Humor was for the weak. "Yeah, we can increase the weight. But your weight, it's gonna come from food. If I could make you taller I would, but I can't. I can make you eat more, though. Fatten you up. Might slow you down, but what do I know? Right, kid?"

"I think Buster is gonna gas early," Keith cracked. "I watch all these videos he posts. People don't see it, but I do. I see him breathing heavy."

"Breathing heavy don't mean he ain't got heavy hands," Benny barked. "Heavy hands, kid. Heavy hands belong to heavyweights."

"Who do you think was better, Foreman or Frazier?"

"I think they were both overrated."

"Crazy talk, Coach. That's nonsense."

"Not nonsense. Truth. I can only speak the truth, the whole truth, and nothing but the truth, so help me Jesus."

"The truth?" Keith sounded surprised. "You lie like a rug. That was a lie you just said."

"Well, I'm telling the truth when I say you need to gain more weight. Two weeks, kid. You got two weeks to gain, at a minimum, fifteen more pounds."

"I gained three pounds this morning. I need to take a shit already."

"We're gonna need to work on that footwork too. Didn't like what I saw in sparring yesterday. Anthony skipped around you like a rope."

"Nonsense. He did not, Coach. Yeah, maybe in the earlier rounds, but I saw it. I led him into it. I got some ideas we can try today. You'll see."

"I see what I see. And right now, I see a skinny punk in my front seat who thinks he sees some hotshot superstar in his own mirror."

"You could at least tell me I'm pretty."

"Pretty? Prettiest thing about you is that pretty little attitude of yours. Too pretty, you ask me."

"Speaking of pretty," Keith recalled. "You see the ass on Dana yesterday? She got almost five hundred likes on the photo she posted."

"Kid, you think I'm looking at asses?" Benny said. "Only ass I'm looking at is your skinny one. And anyways, Dana's just a kid like you. I'm an old man with an old man's mind and an old man's cock. That's why Nesrine married me. Makes her feel younger, she tells me."

"Two weeks is more than enough time."

"You might think that now, kid. You might think that now."

"I think I'm gonna shit myself."

The drive to the gym from the diner was only 2.4 miles according to the map application that was installed on Benny's phone. He knew the drive by heart and knew it was shorter, but for some reason he still plugged its coordinates into this computer that people kept calling a "phone," even though phone calls were the least of this device's abilities. The application always took him the worst possible way too. Yet he always followed the computer, because, at this point, he'd surrendered to technology. *Might as well at this point,* Benny thought when Keith had set it all up for him. Told him it was good for traffic. Other than the map program, Benny also liked to use the Wikipedia app to read about old boxers and World War II history. He didn't have a Wikipedia page himself, though. Didn't think it was strange and wouldn't have even made one had he the knowledge. *Who looks at these things anyways?* he thought.

As he drove along roads he could draw with pencil and paper, the congestion was strong. *Jersey City ain't what it used to be. Too many kids now, with their tattoos and weird face piercings, and six-dollar cups of coffee, and dogs. Why the fuck does everyone have a dog?* he angered himself thinking. *Can't go anywhere without a dog blocking your way.* Nesrine wanted a dog once. He said no. They got a cat, named it Oscar, for De La Hoya.

The gym smelled like body odor, which shouldn't have been the case if Donny had been doing his job. It should have smelled like the expensive cleaning materials that Donny begged Benny to buy last month. But Donny wasn't doing his job. Donny was chatting it up with Dana and for good reason. Dana was a regular at the gym. She took some of the classes, ran on the treadmill with her headphones on, and lifted a couple of weights. She also squatted. She squatted every day in tight workout pants of different colors and variety. She had become a distraction for most of the red-blooded males roaming around Hudson Boxing Gym. And that's because her ass was "otherworldly," as some of the gents might have said. So intense was the circumference of her rear end that a staff meeting had to be called and a breakdown of proper eye conduct was explained by an old, tired, and unhorny gym owner to his young, vibrant, and horny male employees.

Benny no longer thought about women the way these youthful men did. All the girls who came into his gym were just that, girls. Kids. He couldn't look at them the same way these savages did. It wasn't in him. Not much was in him anymore. The only thing left in him was what was left in every fighter: the want to keep fighting another round.

He wore lighter gloves now, but after hours, when the lights were shut off and the people were gone and Nesrine was asleep, he'd hop in the Cadillac, leave the phone at home, and come back to the gym to work the heavy bag. Light but quick was how he worked. Tender wrists his whole career, so he made sure to keep it easy. Keep the ghosts easy. Dancing around the bag, he never pretended he was back in the ring when he closed his eyes. He imagined himself standing over his coffin instead, looking down at himself in the ground. Benny was always looking down on himself. He didn't want the only view to be his corpse's looking up.

In his office, on his desk, were flowers. He remembered immediately why but would have still rather forgot. They were flowers marking the anniversary of his retirement from the world of professional boxing. The flowers were from Nesrine. They had met at one of his amateur fights at a VFW hall in Staten Island. Nesrine was working a concession stand. Got married after Benny retired and bought a little apartment in North Bergen. To this day she looked the same as she ever did to Benny. Her card also was the same as ever. *Happy anniversary, my love.* She was too good of a woman for him. Too good to him. He didn't deserve her. Not for all these years. Not for all these rounds.

Out on the mats, in between the bags and the kids, Benny saw Keith doing push-ups. *Push-ups are good for his tits,* he thought. *But he needs to eat more.* "Keith! Be ready for me in thirty minutes," he ordered from behind his desk.

"I was born ready, Coach!" Keith replied from a push-up position. "A real fighter is born ready!"

They were going to have to work inside the ring today. Out on the mats, Juan was teaching a strength and conditioning class to all the kids who worked those cushy jobs that paid them way too much money but who kept open the doors to Hudson Boxing Gym. Kept open the doors to all these businesses in a city that these kids would have never wanted to live in ten to fifteen years ago. But Benny wasn't a bitter man. He was a "realist" if anyone ever asked him.

Thirty minutes later, Benny was holding his custom punch mitts up in the air for Keith to hit combos. He was holding his hands too high; at eye-level was BENNY on the back of his left hand in a proportionally sized font, SCHULTZ in a compromised, smaller font on the back of his right hand. He was holding the mitts too high because Benny was five-foot-eight and Buster Davis was six-foot-three.

"My jab is feeling good," Keith said.

"What you think and what is might not always be the same," Benny said.

They took a break at the sound of the buzzer. Three-minute rounds today. Hard work.

"Saw the flowers from Nesrine on your desk," Keith remarked. He noticed them because he noticed anything that was different in the gym.

"Yeah . . ." the trainer said to his fighter. "You need to remind me about it too?"

"Sorry, Coach," Keith apologized. "I wasn't trying to be nosy. Just noticed them, was all. They're nice. Nesrine is a nice lady."

"She is a nice lady," Benny said. "She was so nice, I married her. But we're not here to talk about flowers. We're here to work."

"I know," Keith replied. "And let me know if I'm dipping my left shoulder too much when I'm throwing the four?"

After they finished, Keith toweled off, and Benny ate a Snickers bar. *That was good work,* Benny told himself. *But it could have been better.* The trainer and his fighter had decided that tomorrow would be a light day. They both needed it. Keith's knuckles were raw and so was Benny's patience. Too many kids in the gym.

That night, Benny went to the Wooden Lantern. He went to the Wooden Lantern because it was Saturday night. He went every Saturday night not because he liked to drink—Benny hadn't been drunk in years—

but because it was a place where he could think. He was the opposite of most in that he actually liked the taste of alcohol but hated the feeling of being drunk. A light beer could keep him occupied for an hour, while his thoughts could keep him occupied for days. And his thoughts were cheaper.

Saturday night was also the night of the week that Nesrine went out with her friends to that Italian restaurant in town that Benny could never remember the name of. *Vincenzo's? Pietro's? Arturo's?* Didn't matter. What did matter was the leftovers she would bring back with her each time. One of the many things Benny loved about his wife was her generosity. Benny was not a generous man. Sure, he could teach his ring knowledge to a bunch of kids, but if there were seven pennies in his pocket, you best believe they were staying there.

Benny ordered his second light beer in three hours. The bartender didn't care; she trained at Hudson Boxing Gym. Would have given him free drinks if he wanted. But Benny never wanted anything other than to be left alone. *Why break his concentration?* the bartender would think as Benny stared aimlessly at the bowl of popcorn in front him. Yet this stark concentration strangers might have thought they saw in Benny's eyes was anything but. Concentration required a focus on an objective. Benny focused on being out of focus with no objective. Benny wasn't concentrating when he was at the bar at the Wooden Lantern. Benny was trying to forget.

Sometimes it could appear as though Benny were computing hard calculus in his head, or drafting the next big novel, or preparing the outlines of that set of shelves he promised Nesrine he'd build four years ago. This would all be untrue. Benny never thought about these things. Benny thought about only one thing when he was alone. Failure. He could see it in every-thing. He could see failure in the lights at the Wooden Lantern. He could see failure in the faces of the bloated men seated around him. He could see failure in the cars in the parking lot. He saw failure in his reflection in the back bar mirror. Failure wasn't new to Benny. In fact, it was as old as him. He came out feet-first from his mother's vagina. Failure. He was held back in the fourth grade. Failure. He barely graduated high school, spending all his time in front of the mirror shadowboxing and trying to pick up girls. Failure (although at the time, it felt like the only way to win). And winning was something Benny never understood. He felt failure even in victory. *Could have done this better. Could have seen this more. Could have, could have, could have . . .* until he couldn't fill his head anymore with shoulda-coulda-wouldas.

At the bar, sitting among all these other failures, Benny could feel normal. Here and at the gym. The sounds of drunks and the sounds of buzzers—all the same, loud and obnoxious—hurt his ears more than his head, and his ears always hurt his head. Benny, old or young, had forever been fond of silence. Even the sound of leather smacking, or bags being hit, or fighters groaning—that wasn't silence, that was necessity. No, Benny liked the kind of silence that made most people scared. The kind of silence the ocean brings to its whales and fishes and to the people stupid enough to test its powers. The silence that came with dead sleep. *How come no one likes silence?* Benny would think in silence. *Silence is where dreams are made, where dreams die.* His dream had died in silence. Maybe he would to.

He never spoke of these thoughts out loud, for that would ruin the silence he so desperately adored. Nesrine understood. Hell, she could do enough talking for the both of them. Problem was, when Benny talked, he always sounded grumpy even if he wasn't. Even if he was in a good mood (which was rare) or when he wasn't trying to be silent (which was even rarer), his orders and opinions still sounded like a wasp's nest disturbed. But this didn't bother him. Benny was sixty-one years old. Benny had lived well beyond the date of expiration he had printed on himself decades of thoughts prior. "Playing with house money," he'd say to Nesrine over a dinner of sirloin steak, mashed potatoes, and, if he was lucky, and Nesrine was for it, her mother's famous cornbread. But Nesrine was trying to watch her weight. She was eight years younger than her husband, and that never bothered her when her friends questioned her about it when they first started dating or when they questioned her after Benny proposed. She didn't question it now when she slept next to her husband of so many years.

Sitting on the second stool from the far end of the bar, Benny thought about these things while the other people there thought about all the other things Benny could have been thinking about. It was a game being played unbeknownst to anyone playing it.

I don't care about the weight, Benny thought. *It's the power. Kids like him don't have that power. Not born with the same power. Power comes from the tits.*

He almost ordered a third beer but thought better of it, thought, *I need to drive home still.* Benny wasn't drunk, but the low-alcohol beer had provided enough of a stirring in his blood that he knew another one would turn his Cadillac from the boat it was to the barge it could be. A difficult car to drive in the first place, beer only made it worse. Plus another beer would make him feel like when your head smacks the floor after your feet have fallen flat from beneath you. Benny hated that feeling, and he hated being drunk. Thanksgiving 2003. Nesrine's twin sister was in town. She lived in Chile with her Chilean husband, and they brought Chilean wine from Santiago. Benny drank a whole bottle. Felt the thud in his head for a week— almost as long as the last time he had been in the ring. That lasted ten days. He remembered every day. He also knew he had to leave the bar. The things he was thinking he would soon be speaking, and that wouldn't be good for anybody. He paid his tab, thanked the bartender, and thanked god he didn't get pulled over. Nesrine was asleep in bed when he lay down next to her. He closed his eyes and looked forward to good work tomorrow, but his mind kept churning.

Keith Way was a good boxer, but he had fought chumps. A padded record. That was the business, and no one knew the business as well as Benny. Too bad he never made any money doing it. But the business had changed, and Benny didn't like change. But Keith had changed something inside of him whether he liked it or not. What that was he couldn't say, because he didn't know.

Not knowing was one of the worst possibilities for a fighter going out there in the world. *He has no idea what Buster is gonna bring,* he thought. *He has no clue these guys hit different, hurt different, box different.* Anthony Maliganoni might have gone up to heavyweight too, but he hit like a middleweight. Won his first fight and lost his next three, and that's why they were paying him to spar Keith. Because he was a chump and Keith could learn from fighting chumps, *and that's why he shouldn't go up in fucking weight!* Benny almost yelled out loud. Benny didn't want Keith to lose any fights, and if he stayed in his weight class, he wouldn't. Benny didn't want Keith to learn about failure in the ring. It was too important of a lesson to be taught with gloves on.

When the trainer woke up, the fighter was in his kitchen. He looked a little thick in the belly sitting on a kitchen stool and that put Benny in a good mood immediately. *If only he had tits,* he thought. Benny woke up every morning at 6:54 A.M. He hadn't used an alarm clock for he forgot how long. He woke up when he woke up because, he believed, "that's the only time my body ever gives me the answer I'm looking for." He wasn't wrong in the same way Keith wasn't right when he asked, "Just cardio today, right, Coach?"

Benny ignored him, his universal answer for "no," and Keith understood in the way a family member of a mute understands: it was in his eyes; if he could talk, he probably wouldn't say anything anyway. Nesrine yelled something from the bedroom. What it was didn't matter, because if it were important, she would have made sure Benny heard it. There was coffee made. Benny poured a cup. Drove with the cup and Keith in the Cadillac to the diner, then the gym. Drank from the cup at his desk. He never spilled a drip of coffee from his cup. Ever.

Donny was stoned. Benny was sure of it, but he didn't care. It was 2019. There were worse things to worry about than the manager of your place of business smoking a joint before he opened at seven A.M.

Rap music was playing on the stereo system. It should have been Black Sabbath, but Benny didn't arrive at the gym until two hours after it opened, and this was the shit the kids listened to nowadays. Music to make you want to put a gun in your mouth. His whole life Benny liked nothing but hard and fast music. Punk, metal, thrash—this was the music that got him into the gym when he was a kid, got him excited to lift weights in the air and smash them on the ground. Smash faces. Be a fighter.

"I want you sweating before I finish taking this shit!" Benny yelled at his fighter. His words snaked around the class Emmanuel was teaching. "Old-School Boxing," Benny had named it. Not because the techniques were old but because only the old members of the gym took it.

Benny went to his private bathroom that was behind his office. There were two more bathrooms out in the gym area, one for the girls and one for the boys, but Benny needed his privacy. He had caught an old employee using his bathroom to take a shit once. He fired him and bought a new toilet. *I've taken it up the ass my whole life. Let me at least have my own place to shit it all out,* he rationalized to himself. He'd had a digestive problem a couple of years back. He went to the doctor and the doctor said it was stress. Benny never heard of stress being able to make someone not shit and went to get an enema instead. He told Nesrine he got a root canal. Benny liked having his own toilet.

"Where are my mitts?" Benny questioned when he came out of the bathroom. "Donny, where the fuck are my mitts?"

Everything in his gym was supposed to be in its

rightful place, always. If it wasn't, then that was bad news for whoever misplaced it, because Benny hated when things were not where he thought they were. He wanted to be able to sleepwalk through his gym and know where every jump rope, computer cable, tea bag, and spit bucket was. This was considered "order," and order was what Benny liked because that was part of what made a good fighter. Order and a thousand other things that Keith Way thought he would have at heavy-weight but already had at cruiserweight. *And the kid still didn't have a sweat!*

The next class was soon shuffling in through the door, and that eased Benny's mind. He knew what really kept his business afloat. Sure, Keith might have made a nice purse or two, from which Benny was able to use his portion of swiftly, but that's not what paid the gym's bills. What kept the lights open were the kids who came morning and night for the classes that Hudson Boxing Gym offered. He charged a lot of money for a membership, $185 a month, but that included unlimited classes. A steal, if you asked him, for a bunch of kids who didn't know any better. Thing was, the same thirty to forty people took all the classes. New blood came and went to work sparring, but the hardcores were what mattered, because they were the names on the credit cards, names that Benny had memorized. Whenever the holidays came around, or when he and Nesrine took their yearly vacation down to Florida to visit her brother in West Palm Beach, or when he splurged on dessert after an expensive dinner, it was the names on these Visas and Discovers and Mastercards (but not American Express) that locked into sequence to unlock the bolt to his heart. Money ruled the roost only because Benny never made a lot of it. Not that money would have made him happier, but it would have made it easier to not be so driven by his fear of failure. *Rich people lose their drive,* Benny thought. *I don't want to lose my drive. I can't afford to.* And that's why Benny wasn't rich. Because he thought things that weren't true, even if they might have been.

Keith was practicing his left hook in the mirror. "He's gonna need it," Benny said under his breath. Keith fought in a traditional stance, or in other words, he was a "righty." That meant the power of his left hook came from his left foot. And his left foot was pivoting the way Benny liked.

The overhead lights in the gym buzzed mechanically, almost in rhythm to the sounds of the kids slamming kettle bells and knocking speedbags. "Hard work equals positive results!" Benny screamed at them as he walked around and through, forward and back, until he was satisfied they all knew he was there. He'd have painted the words on the walls, but he thought better of it. He hung up a poster of Roberto Durán instead. Thankfully none of these kids working their combos in the mirror and practicing punches thrown at shadows knew who Keith Way was. And that's because *Keith Way fought bums,* Benny thought. Keith was just another guy who worked out in that other part of the gym near the ring that the kids who paid for classes never ventured to. Where the weights that no one lifted existed. Where the machines that no one used lived. This part of the gym was for the kids "who think they're fighters," Benny would say. *It was where work got done,* Benny would think. He liked that part of the gym in the way he liked the Wooden Lantern. He liked it in the way he liked his Cadillac. He liked it in the way he liked Nesrine's cooking. It was comfortable. Nothing better for a fighter.

"I don't see you working, kid!"

"Coach," Keith said. "Stepped on the scale this morning. 194 pounds."

"That's good, kid. But not good enough."

"It's not good enough. But it's good enough for government work."

"You really say that to people?" Benny asked his fighter. *If he says that now, what's he gonna say if he wins?*

Donny had laced Keith's gloves this morning. "I don't think Donny laced me tight enough, Coach."

Donny hadn't, but they were already running twelve minutes behind, and Benny didn't like to run behind. "You watch that tape I gave you last week?"

"Not yet, Coach. I don't own a VHS player. To be honest, I don't think anyone has since, like, 2004."

"Goddammit, kid! What good is it if I give you the goods but you do nothing good with it?"

"It was probably focused around his right hook."

"Of course it was! He's got a vicious hook, kid. Can knock you clear out."

"But I'll be seeing his punches from miles away."

"Do I have to slap the sense into you myself?"

"Let's work, Coach. I'm golden."

Benny held his custom-embroidered mitts high, but after a minute of holding the gloves at this level, his shoulders began to hurt. He ignored the pain to not show his weakness, although Keith couldn't have cared less. Keith would have preferred it actually, because he thought Benny had been holding the mitts too high, but he didn't want to say anything and bruise the ego of the old man. Too easy to bruise an old trainer.

Bouncing around the ring, Benny and Keith worked on slips. Slips were important, as a good slip meant a good chance of not getting hit, and that was what boxing was all about to Benny. *If I had known that then, I wouldn't be here now*, he thought.

"You keep moving flat on your left foot, kid!"

"Flat? What are you talking about?"

"Did I stutter? Flat, kid. Your fucking foot is flat when you move. Look!" Benny pointed at his fighter's feet.

"But we're not moving, Coach."

"You're always moving in boxing, kid."

They did good enough work for Benny to not bring it home with him. The drive home did a great job throwing the junk of his mind away, but there was traffic, and this junked up Benny's mood instead. Jersey

City was a traffic jam 24/7. *What the fuck happened to this city?* he wondered. *What happened to this place?*

Nesrine and Benny's apartment building had one parking space included per unit. Unfortunately, both he and Nesrine had cars. Nesrine worked a bit of a drive north in the township of Mahwah. Benny liked Mahwah. Liked the small industrial park that his wife worked in. Good pizza, good bagels, and high taxes. Made New Jersey almost worth living in. Benny enjoyed when things were good. Life ran smooth when things were good. "Perfection in smoothness," he'd say. Benny parked his Cadillac on the street.

"Hey, honey!"

Benny always put his keys on the little shelf inside the front doorway of their small apartment. "Hey, babe," he said, and placed his keys where they should always be if they weren't on his person.

"I made pork loins tonight!"

Fuck, Benny cursed. "Sounds great, babe!" he said to his wife.

"You look tired. Did Keith put in some good work today?"

"Some might call it that."

Benny sat down at the small kitchen table inside their small kitchen. When Keith was there, he'd fill the room like an elephant. When he wasn't, the talk of him did.

"How's your shoulder?"

Rubbing it, he said, "It's been better."

"Paulie called the house phone earlier."

"What did he want? Why didn't he call me on my cell phone?"

"He wanted to know if you could meet him for breakfast in Hoboken tomorrow."

"Why can't we go to the Empress Diner?"

"Why are you asking me?"

"I'll call him back."

Benny went into the small living room of their small apartment and pulled out his large iPhone. He forgot the passcode and felt a jump in his heart for a beat; proof of how ingrained this new technology was in this old trainer's life. *What if I locked myself out?* he worried, but then he remembered that Keith had set it all up for him and held all the passcodes and passwords and whatever the fuck he needed to remember for this device but couldn't. Then he remembered that his phone held nothing of importance. That what was important to him was inside that kitchen cooking the devil's meat. Then he remembered his passcode. It was his birthday, 2558.

"Paulie, you call?"

Paulie Pasquale was Benny's oldest friend in the world. They had grown up together on the streets of Jersey City, terrorizing the neighbors with typical kid mischief and innocent pranks in days of innocence. City kids. Paulie's father—a city kid grown up—had been a street guy who got mixed up with an Italian family on the other side of the Hudson and was shot dead in front of an eleven-year-old Paulie as they were leaving a Chinese restaurant one night. His father left behind a debt, a wife, and three kids. Paulie was the youngest and got picked on a lot, and that's why Benny immediately liked him. Liked the toughness Paulie was forced to grow. It made Benny feel tough. And fighters were supposed to be tough. Paulie was also co-owner of Hudson Boxing Gym and Keith Way's cutman. Paulie was what Benny needed, even if Benny thought what he needed was Keith. Keith knew Benny and Paulie needed each other. Nesrine knew everything.

"How's the kid looking?" Paulie asked into Benny's ear.

"He needs to eat more."

"Speaking of eating, how's about breakfast tomorrow? Let's go to Brenda's."

"Why can't we go to the Empress?"

"Because their coffee is garbage and their food is even worse."

"I hate Hoboken," Benny complained. "Too many kids there."

"I'll see you at seven thirty," Paulie said.

Benny hung up the phone. When he went back into the kitchen, Nesrine had dinner on the table. The pork loins looked good, but Benny didn't like eating pork because of "Jewish guilt," he'd tell himself, although he hadn't stepped foot inside of a synagogue since his bar mitzvah. But he always ate whatever Nesrine cooked with a smile because that was what

Nesrine brought to his face every day. He knew the world needed more smiles. He was just grateful for the small ones he could catch himself.

The next morning, traffic was junked up on John F. Kennedy Boulevard, and the only thing Benny hated more than traffic was Brenda's parking situation. *"No fucking parking anywhere in this goddamn fucking city,"* he'd scream under his breath. His anger used to be worse, though. One time he got so angry over a parking spot at Brenda's, he punched the steering wheel of his Cadillac. American engineering slugged him back and broke his knuckle. He told Nesrine some kid dropped a weight on his hand by accident.

"You see the tits on Buster Davis?" Benny asked his oldest friend in the world.

"Great tits. I've seen some good tits, but that boy's got some of the best."

"Kid won't eat. I keep trying to get him to eat more. Anything."

"How's that cut healed?"

"What cut?"

"Don't play fool with me, Benny."

"Cut's fine."

Keith had been cut in sparring three weeks prior. It wasn't a big cut, but it was a cut, and cuts were no good in boxing.

"He'll make the weight," Paulie told his friend. "You're always worrying."

"Well, someone has to fucking worry!"

"You getting the pork chops?"

"Paulie, let me ask you something."

"Anything, Benny."

"Why do you think he's doing it?"

"Why do I think who is doing what?"

"Do I have to explain everything to you? Why is Keith moving up weight?"

"Because no one cares about the cruiserweight champion of the world."

"But no one is gonna care about Keith after he loses this fight."

"How're you so sure he's going to lose this fight?"

"You see Buster's tits?!" Benny screamed.

Paulie ordered steak and eggs, and Benny ordered two scrambled eggs with whole wheat toast. In contrast to how much food he wanted his fighter to eat, Benny's doctor said he could afford to lose a few pounds himself. Nesrine bought him whole wheat bread the next day. He hated the taste of it at first, hated the change. But then he got used to it. Pretty soon it started to taste no different from the white bread he knew so well. Then he forgot he used to eat white bread at all. Then he forgot that he had changed.

Paulie and Benny split the bill because they both owned the same gym and thus the same income source. They, in turn, owned each other.

They walked over to the Cadillac. The passenger-side door was hard to open. Got stuck. Benny didn't care because he was never a passenger in his own car.

Benny liked to be in control. Paulie managed to pry the door open and got in.

As Benny drove, he flipped the radio on; a Frank Sinatra song was playing. Benny loved theses old-timey tunes even if he wasn't old enough to like them. Benny and Paulie, almost born on the same day of the same year, had been born after the bad got good and before the good got bad: after the Nazis rampaged Europe and before the hippies burned out America. Two players born on the wrong base, their childhood felt like one big fight. That's why their middle school gym coach put them in a boxing ring. Put them up against some real kids who could fight. Paulie got pummeled and Benny held his own. Paulie played baseball and Benny kept fighting. Paulie went to college and Benny kept fighting. Paulie got a job and Benny kept fighting. Paulie wanted a family and Benny lost. Paulie and Benny then opened Hudson Boxing Gym.

"If your fighter heard you talk the way I do, he'd never fight," Paulie said as the Cadillac pulled into the parking lot of Hudson Boxing Gym.

"I talk all the time! The kid just doesn't listen."

Donny was hitting on a lesbian couple who came in only on Monday mornings for Kara's recovery class when Paulie and Benny walked in. "Ooohhhh! Look who it is!"

Paulie didn't spend a lot of time at the gym, maybe stopped by twice a week. After his heart attack, Paulie didn't work as much, but the gym was making good money with all the classes it offered, and Paulie's wife, Sherla, had gotten promoted at her job too. Paulie liked to play solitaire nowadays and watch PGA golf on TV. He didn't like to hang out in boxing gyms.

"Donny!" Paulie cheered. "See you're hard at work as always."

Donny looked back at the lesbian couple whose asses both held their own gravitational pull. "You call this work?"

"Benny," Paulie called out, "let me know when Keith is ready."

"I'm always ready," Keith said from behind his shoulder.

"Thought I smelled you."

The two embraced. Benny only hugged Nesrine.

"How's the cut?"

"Cut is only what you make of it, Paulie."

"That doesn't make any sense, but if you say so."

"Nothing I'm gonna have to worry about for the fight. Buster ain't gonna come at me with the left hand."

"He's not, is he?"

"Nope. Been watching all his training videos on Instagram."

"On what?"

"On Instagram. He has over two hundred thousand followers."

"Benny!" Paulie shouted over the rap that plagued

the gym's stereo system most hours of the day. "What the fuck is an Instapan?"

"Instagram," Keith corrected.

"That's great, Keith. Go lace up. We got work to do."

Donny laced up Keith's gloves while Benny and Paulie went in the gym's office. Although they both owned the gym, Benny took over the sole office because Paulie wouldn't have otherwise. Benny liked the office because he could close the door. It was the only door in his entire existence that he could keep closed and nobody would bother him. *Botheration is a liability,* Benny would think. "Botheration gets in the way of good work," he'd say. On the back of Benny's office door hung a piece of paper. Written on it was STAY SHARP, EAT RIGHT, AND MAKE GOOD DECISIONS. He liked that sign because when he saw it, it meant his door was closed.

"You see his tits?" Benny asked his oldest friend in the world.

"Will you please stop?" Paulie said, sitting down on the other side of Benny's desk and taking a mini Snickers bar from the bowl of candy that survived next to the photo of Nesrine that lived on Benny's desk. "His tits look fine."

"I don't know, Paulie. Buster Davis is a big boy. Can't get that big this soon."

"Bigger isn't always better, Benny."

"Sure it ain't."

"How's membership numbers next month looking?"

"You're asking me? I don't know. I'm here for the fighters! Ask Donny."

"You need to be here for everyone," Paulie said.

"I'm here, I'm here. Enough of this. Let's go do work."

Benny climbed into the ring. He liked to enter between the second and third ropes, not because he was a shorter man, but because that's how he learned. Teaching this old dog a new trick would have been pointless. It would have been change. Pointless. Keith was bouncing in the corner and talking to Paulie. It was going to be a morning of combinations. *The kid is too slow with that counter cross,* Benny thought. *Buster Davis has a nasty counter. If he doesn't see it coming, then we got no chance. Boxing is movement. If you don't move, you get hit.* Getting hit wasn't in Benny's game plan for Keith because he knew how hard Buster Davis could hit. Keith knew too but in a different way. Keith knew how hard Buster Davis could hit through the screen of his phone.

Benny met Keith in the middle of the ring. "All right, kid. Let's start with a one-two-three-two, but I want you slipping after that last two. Buster's got a monstrous right counter."

"Big counter," Paulie agreed from the corner.

They worked the combo for a couple of minutes until Benny was satisfied with his fighter in the way one is satisfied of hunger after eating a large popcorn and soda at the movies. Mildly.

"Don't forget his hook to the body too, kid. He's got height on you."

Buster Davis was six-foot-three. Boxing liked tall heavyweights. The world liked tall heavyweights. *The world doesn't need Keith Way to be its heavyweight champion.* Benny knew this even if his fighter didn't.

"Harder, kid!" he screamed. Benny held his mitt down low by his right hip with his right hand flipped over. "Four to the body! Good, kid. Again."

"Looking good from over here, guys!" Paulie screamed.

"Here too!" Donny said on his stroll to the bathroom.

"They're morons," Benny said to his fighter. "*Good* is not good enough in boxing."

"That doesn't make any sense, but if you say so," Keith said, repeating what he'd heard earlier.

"Jab!" Benny demanded. "*Good* isn't going to put fifteen more pounds on your body."

"I ate three Twinkies right before we got in here."

They hopped and boogied around the ring and around the clock long enough for Benny to catch a sweat. That's when he knew it was time for a break. "Guys wanna go to the Empress?" he asked his compatriots. "I'll drive."

On the way over to the Empress Diner, Benny's phone rang. It was Nesrine. She was free and wanted to know if he'd like to have lunch with her. He told her he was having lunch with Paulie and Benny and that she should come join them. No one in the Cadillac blinked an eye at the suggestion, because they knew Benny was nothing without Nesrine. They knew that in the way you knew that Monday would always follow Sunday. How nine would always follow eight. How a dumb man should always follow a good woman.

She was sitting in Benny's favorite booth when they arrived.

"The three most handsome men in all of New Jersey," she said upon their entrance, "and they're having lunch with me!" She kissed Benny on the side of the cheek. "I made sure they had whole wheat."

"They always have whole wheat! That's why I come here."

"Nesrine," Paulie said from across the table, "looking beautiful as always."

Keith sat next to him. "Hey, Mrs. Schultz."

"Don't let him tell you that you need to keep eating, Keith," she said.

"He does!" Benny yelled. "Look at his tits!"

Nesrine rolled her eyes. "Paulie, how is Sherla? Been meaning to call her for the last couple of days. Work has been crazy."

"She's good. Melissa, though. That girl is going to put me in an early grave."

Benny and Nesrine never had kids. Not because they couldn't, but because they didn't want to. And this decision, made early on in their relationship, had put them into a different category of "friend" for most of their friends. They never regretted their decision. They enjoyed each other enough. Conversing about braces or SAT tutors was never going to be part of their life. It also saved them from conversations like these.

"Keith," Benny said, interrupting Paulie, "you should get the special today."

"What is it?"

"Meat lover's omelet."

"Yeah, okay."

Just a kid, Benny thought. And he was right. Keith Way was like every single other kid Benny saw walking around his city. Another idiot staring at his phone. And here was his fighter looking up on his phone the reviews of the Empress Diner's meat lover's omelet.

"Put that goddamn thing away!"

"Coach, you got to see this." He handed his phone to Benny with the screen showing Buster Davis's Instagram page. "He just posted this video of him and his trainer working at Gleason's."

"Let me see that," Benny said, and stared hard at the phone.

Benny wanted to see how clean the inside of Gleason's Gym was more than he wanted to see Buster Davis train. A notification from @phattyphatpat2344_12 came on the screen before he could finish the video. Benny instinctively clicked it. *"Love yur last fgiht bro! U at HeavywEight gonna be epik! Kick Buter's ASS!"*

"I think someone sent you something," Benny said.

"Haha, yeah," Keith said as he looked at his phone. "That dude comments on everything I post." This particular post was a picture of Keith eating cheeseburgers at White Manna in Hackensack.

"Keith, how are you feeling about the fight?" Nesrine asked. She asked because she genuinely cared. She'd lived her whole life around fighters. Her own mother fought breast cancer—twice—and won.

"I feel great, Mrs. Schultz! I—"

"Stop calling her that!" Benny snapped. "She doesn't like that. Call her Nesrine."

"Don't listen to him," Nesrine said. "Grumpy bastard."

"Sorry. Habit. I'm feeling good about the fight, Mrs. Schultz. I'm gonna be lighter than Buster, but not by much. Pack on some more muscle once I get past him."

"Muscle. That's what you need, kid," the trainer said to his fighter. "More muscle. The fight is less than two weeks away!"

"Tits are looking pretty good," Paulie said. "Not yours, Nesrine. Keith's. Sorry. You know what I meant."

"Thanks," Keith said. "Did you know that Tyson was the same height as me, Mrs. Schultz?"

"Mike Tyson? I did not know that."

"Tyson?! You're talking about Mike Tyson?" Benny screamed.

A child in the booth over appeared concerned. Not

for Benny, but for the people sitting around him. *He screams like my dad,* the child thought.

"Tyson was a bulldog born in the gutter. He also weighed 225 pounds! You were born in Ridgewood."

"Great tits on Tyson," Paulie said.

Nesrine nodded her head in agreement because it was true.

The waitress came over. *Same waitress as the other day?* Benny thought, but, unsure, didn't say anything to avoid the embarrassment. If it was the same girl, she should know Benny wanted whole wheat for everything, because Benny was a whole wheat kind of guy. But he knew she wouldn't recognize him, and he knew he would now need to go through the necessary motions of the question-answer conversation that eating at a restaurant with humans who served you came with. Benny had ordered on a machine in McDonald's a couple of days prior. He preferred it that way.

Benny ordered first. "I'll have the cajun chicken wrap on—"

"Would you like that on a plain or whole wheat wrap?"

"He'll have it on the whole wheat wrap," Nesrine answered.

"I was going to tell her that!" Benny yelled. "Whole wheat wrap. Always whole wheat. And a side of bacon."

"You don't need bacon," Nesrine whispered into Benny's ear.

"And you, honey?" the waitress asked Keith.

"I'll have the meat lover's omelet."

"Make it two," Benny said.

"What? Nah, Coach. I can't eat that much. You're crazy."

"Buster Davis eats meat lover's omelets in his sleep!"

"Can I have the Reuben?" Paulie said.

"Reuben?" Benny asked him. "It's not even noon."

"Is there a time that one must eat a Reuben after?"

"It sure as fuck ain't before noon!"

"And you, ma'am?" the waitress asked Nesrine.

"I'll take the Reuben too."

Benny snorted.

An hour later and they had finished their meal. *An hour at a diner is the perfect amount of time,* Benny always thought. *Unless you're by yourself. Then it should be no longer than thirty minutes,* he'd say if you asked. But no one ever asked him.

———

The gym felt humid as he walked inside the bathroom on a busy Thursday morning. "Donny! Why are there no paper towels?" Benny screamed at the gym's manager.

The sink in Benny's bathroom busted earlier that

week. But instead of hiring a plumber, he and Donny watched a video on YouTube and figured they could do it themselves. They couldn't. They had actually made it worse. The plumber was coming next week. In the meantime, Benny had been forced to wash his hands in the men's bathroom out in the gym.

Part of Donny's job was to maintain the bathrooms. That meant stocking paper towels. And in a boxing gym, there was a lot to clean up with paper towels other than wet hands: bloody noses, bloody eyes, bloody egos. But instead of working and stocking, Donny was on YouTube showing Elizabeth a video of a guy on a mountain bike being chased by a bear.

Elizabeth was the gym's newest employee, hired to teach technique classes in that part of the gym where the weights were that no one ever used. Fresh blood kept old clientele, which was crucial, and Benny, out of tendency to the obvious, hired only attractive people. This wasn't because he liked to look at them, but because most attractive people were usually in shape. And the reason most attractive people were in shape was because *they have little else to offer the world*, Benny thought. Low self-worth was easier to deal with if you could conceal the emptiness that existed inside you by outwardly displaying box jumps, juice cleanses, and 140 minutes on the treadmill. But he didn't hire them for their conversational skills either. Clients liked to take lessons from attractive people. "Half the reason they even come to the gym," Benny would say to

Nesrine in bed at night. And this was true. Mirrors reflecting back their swollen bodies, the people paying his monthly nut liked to catch a glimpse of a girl wearing impossibly delicious workout pants and a set of pink Cleto Reyes gloves to take their mind off the clock and their own grossness.

The plan for today was to work the heavy bag for six three-minute rounds, take a lunch, and then work free weights and another six three-minute-round session with mitts. Unfortunately, Benny was training his fighter in a handicapped manner. He knew that, and Keith knew that. There wasn't the money for a professional training camp at this level of "professional" competition. Sure, Keith Way might have been undefeated, "but he'd only fought bums," Benny would say if you asked him. "And he ain't a champ yet." Since money didn't exist, Benny had to be traditional in his training techniques, and that meant traditional exercises and routines. It had been that way from the start, so Keith was used to it, knew in his head they'd move beyond this once he moved beyond Buster Davis. "One day at a time" had always been Keith Way's motto. *"Today is today, let tomorrow wait,"* he preached on an Instagram post a couple of days ago. If Keith Way posted something, then he meant it.

"It's not the camp that makes the fighter. It's the fighter that makes the camp," Benny would tell Keith before his earlier bouts. And they'd won every one. *We must be doing something right,* they both thought.

The trainer and his fighter worked hard those first six rounds, but both men began to fade in the later session. This made sense to Benny, because Benny wasn't fighting Buster Davis. Keith Way was fighting Buster Davis. Good thing too, because Benny's right shoulder had been bothering him. But like a boxer, he worked through it. *You gotta work through pain in boxing. Boxing is supposed to be painful.* Maybe that's why Benny loved the sport so much. He loved an already painful thing so much that he was able to make it hurt worse. He could make his defeat worse, too. Make it crush him. He didn't want Keith Way to get crushed like he did. Keith could hit, Benny wouldn't deny that. And he could move. But he needed to eat more, and more time was something they couldn't order off a menu. More time was something Benny had never found on a menu in any diner in all of New Jersey. That "daily special" didn't exist. *More time doesn't exist.*

"All right, kid! Let's wrap this up. I need to hit the sack," Benny said. "Slept like shit last night."

Keith felt good about their work and had no problems finishing up ahead of schedule for the day. Plus, now he could spend a little more time watching *Game of Thrones*. He had picked up the show only recently and had been watching it with any available free time.

This was usually right before falling asleep each night. The sounds of death and dragons put him to sleep quicker than the sounds of silence that surrounded him every night, as Keith no longer lived in the town he grew up in but had moved to the even sleepier suburb of Allendale. He rented a small two-bedroom house he couldn't really afford and lived alone. Sabrina, his girlfriend of two years, would spend a couple of nights there each week, but during a training camp, he would forbid her from staying over. Keith Way firmly believed in denying himself the pleasure of an orgasm before a fight, for four to six weeks usually. No sex, or oral, or masturbation. He believed in building up his supply of testosterone. He hadn't lost a fight yet. Keith Way was 12-0 in the cruiserweight division. Why question anything now?

Benny drove his Cadillac from the gym to the Wooden Lantern. It was Saturday night, after all, and the light beer would help him sleep heavier. Benny had always been a light sleeper, but construction had kept him up the night before. "When the fuck did they start doing work at midnight?" Benny had shouted at Nesrine in bed like it was her fault. Outside their third-story window, two trucks were cutting down trees and installing power lines in the middle of the night, and now, today, Benny felt like shit because of it. He and his fighter still did good work, but it could have been better. *Could always be better.* And tonight, Benny would sleep better because he had to. Poor sleep was worse than catching a cold at his age. He also no longer woke up with erections, not for years. He was in his sixties. Hadn't had an erection without a pill for a decade. But he woke up fresh every morning. To wake up fresh signified the same status of his inner being that waking up with an erection used to. It would be a means for good work. To wake up groggy meant it would be a hard day of good work. But it would be good work. Always.

The Wooden Lantern was jam-packed when Benny pulled into the parking lot. His spot, in the farthest corner, was open, though, so Benny gunned the accelerator. The car jolted forward as he sped into the spot and slammed the big car into park. "Got it!" he exulted out loud to himself. He felt unsure whether tonight would be a good night to go to the bar. He didn't like crowds. Crowds meant idiots, and Benny couldn't stand idiots. But he decided to go in anyway simply because Nesrine wasn't home and he didn't quite feel like being alone at this moment. He couldn't figure out why, since he usually loved being alone, but tonight he couldn't. *Maybe because I slept like shit,* he thought as he approached the front entrance. That wasn't it, though. The fatigue had left him after noon. Benny could fight through fatigue. Any fighter can fight through fatigue. They must. Rather, it was the anxiousness he felt about his fighter. About his fight. About defeat. Why Benny couldn't get defeat off his mind he didn't know. It had been there ever since he had felt it himself. It had been years. And like peeling a Band-Aid off your skin a millimeter at a time, the sting of it had lasted longer than it should have.

Inside the bar was a party. A party for whom, Benny couldn't tell, as there were no balloons or a birthday cake, but then he saw Gerry McConnell at the end of the bar surrounded by a group of men dressed in Adidas tracksuits. Gerry was the owner of Hobo Boxing in Hoboken. You could call him direct competition to Hudson Boxing Gym, but that wouldn't have been accurate. They were in different cities. The proximity they held to each other was not much of a factor, as most of their clients bitched about having to walk six blocks to the nearest Whole Foods anyway. Their rivalry fell inside the ring, not outside of it.

Hobo Boxing was home to the IBF middleweight champion Darius Booker. Darius Booker was twenty-eight years old, stood five-foot-nine, weighed 157 pounds, and used to train at Hudson Boxing Gym. He was a punk when he first came to the gym. Begged Benny to train him. After winning a couple of amateur fights with Benny in his corner, Darius knocked up his girlfriend and was forced to move to Union City from Irvington. He had promised Benny, "This move ain't shit, Coach," which Benny knew was a lie; the trainer knew this fighter would be history. History to him at least. *He isn't a real fighter,* Benny said to himself. Then, after a couple months of living, Benny didn't see Darius at the gym anymore. He didn't have a fight scheduled, but usually the kid liked to keep in shape between bouts. And then Benny ran into Gerry McConnell one morning at a bagel shop a year or so later. And Darius Booker was there too. And they were both wearing Hobo Boxing sweatshirts. Benny needed no further explanation.

Now at the Wooden Lantern all these years later, Benny saw Gerry. And then he saw Darius walking out of the bathroom. And then it all made sense. Before Benny could leave, Gerry screamed, "Look at this fuck who just walked in!" over Journey playing on the jukebox.

Fuck.

Darius looked at the ground like he did every time he ran into Benny.

Benny walked over because he had to. He could have run out the door, but then he'd be running away from . . . he didn't even know what anymore. Benny directed his attention toward Darius. "How goes it, champ?"

"It's good, Coach."

Benny laughed nervously. "Not your coach anymore, kid."

"Heard your guy's got a big fight coming up," Gerry interjected. "Moving up too?"

"Heavyweight," Benny answered. "Kid needs to eat more."

Benny didn't dislike Gerry. He couldn't, because Gerry wasn't a bad guy. In fact, he was a really nice guy and an exceptional trainer, if you had asked Benny, but no one did, so Benny never said anything about it. Benny, however, did not care for Darius. But he understood the business of congeniality and the currency it held in northern New Jersey.

"This one won't stop eating," Gerry said about his fighter. "Ain't tall enough for super middleweight either."

"Ain't shit, Gerry," Darius said.

Benny thought it strange Darius didn't call Gerry "Coach" but by his real name instead. "What's the celebration for?" he asked.

"Darius just got the call for a shot at the WBC belt," Gerry said.

"No shit?" Benny asked. He felt excited for them, which was out of character for him. He needed a beer.

"Yeah. But Darius's agent isn't sure we should take it just yet," Gerry said.

"Punk ass don't know shit," Darius argued.

Benny knew nothing of agents and managers and sponsors that weren't local. The ignorance made him feel stupid, and that made him feel angry, and that made him sad. "Well, hope it all works out, kid," he said. "Gonna settle down for a quick one. Enjoy your party, gentlemen."

"When's the fight?" Gerry asked before Benny could walk away.

"Next Saturday."

"Newark Veterans Memorial Coliseum?"

"Yeah."

"We'll be there," Gerry said.

Fuck, Benny cursed to himself.

He ordered a light beer and was happy to sit at the farthest possible stool from Hobo Boxing's get-together. Benny, never one for parties to begin with, didn't need this tonight. Benny wanted to think by himself, but now his head was clouded with other thoughts and not thoughts of boxing and uppercuts and electricity bills. His new thoughts were of life, of years gone. Thoughts of mortality. He knew the end was coming. *Not yet,* he told himself, *but sooner than you think.* Benny wasn't a morbid man, but he was aware that he was here for only so long. He'd owned his business for over twenty years, married a beautiful and thoughtful woman, and still had his health and his hair. Death didn't scare him because he held few regrets. "People afraid of dying are the same people afraid of living," he'd say if you asked him. But everywhere Benny looked, he couldn't not see tints of failure in it all. Failure in the bartender, failure in the Cadillac, failure in everything. And Benny strived for excellence in everything. He was blind to all else.

The beer was warm. It was in a bottle, obviously straight from the case it arrived in, and since this was Benny's one night of the week, he wanted a cold beer. *What the fuck's the point of drinking a warm beer?* The bar was extra crowded because of the party on the other end of it, and even with the extra help behind the bar, the bartenders were still busy. Although upset with a warm beer in his hand, he still knew enough to not make a big deal out of it. But he also wanted a new one.

"Excuse me," he said to the bartender nearest him, his hand raised in that way young people with inexperience at bars raise their hands when trying to order a drink. She dutifully ignored him, and this relieved Benny. It would give him a chance to rethink his approach. He said, "Excuse me," one more time, but with a softer tone and a harder hand.

Holding two bottles of the same beer that Benny hoped to order, the bartender countered with, "What can I get ya?"

"I'll take one more of those. But cold this time."

The bartender knew he was right and smiled. She knew he had her. *Didn't think he'd say anything,* she thought. "You got it," she said to Benny. She handed him one of the beers already in her hand. "My name is Ida. This one's on me."

Benny hadn't had a woman introduce herself to him since his fighting days. That's why he didn't say his name back in response. He simply forgot. Ida walked away not angry or upset, but just confused. Benny confused a lot of people, but he never confused himself. In the gym, or in the Cadillac, or with Nesrine, or at the Empress Diner, confusion wasn't part of the equation. He was a man who always knew what he wanted. And he had wanted a cold beer and to be alone in a room surrounded by strangers. But then he saw Gerry McConnell and Darius Booker. And then he got served a warm beer. And then he was rude. But now that was over. He could look forward to the rest of his evening. He could—

Benny's phone beeped. It was a text message from Keith Way. It was a link to an Instagram photo. Benny didn't have an Instagram account, so when he pressed on the link, it brought him to a web page. On the web page was a picture of Buster Davis drinking a vegetable smoothie. Benny turned his phone off.

———

The next morning brought about more traffic and the guy at the bagel store putting cheese on his bacon and egg sandwich.

"Harder, kid!" the trainer screamed at his fighter.

"Happy with that weight this morning?" Keith asked between jab-jab-cross drills.

Keith had weighed 202 pounds when they weighed him this morning. But that was immediately after a breakfast burrito and everything bagel with cream cheese. They were a week out and Keith barely weighed the two-hundred-pound heavyweight weight limit. Benny didn't like how Keith's tits looked. And tits were everything to a boxer in Benny's eyes. *Tits are everything.*

"What's there to be happy about?" Benny

answered. "I don't see why I'd have a reason to be happy."

On top of the traffic and cheesy egg sandwich, Donny had arrived late and opened the gym late and set the schedules off for all the classes that Hudson Boxing Gym offered by twenty minutes. Nothing made Benny angrier than not being on time. He despised being late, other people being late, or anything involving the punctuality of others being out of his control. He had lived through the hippies and '80s. "Reliability is a resource to harness, not reject," Benny would say if you had asked him. Benny was never late.

"You see that photo I sent you last night? The one with Buster Davis?"

"I did," Benny said. He didn't want to expand further on it. *What is there to talk about?* he thought. *Fucking guy was drinking a smoothie.* "You have tits like Buster Davis, you can drink all the veggie smoothies you want, kid."

"Yo, Benny!" Donny shouted. "The plumber's on the phone. Said he could squeeze you in today."

Benny looked at the clock. It was 10:46 A.M. "What time?" he asked the gym's manager, who was late this morning and probably stoned.

"He says now."

Fuck. He had just started the day's work with Keith and would have to leave early to go with Nesrine to Upper Saddle River for her boss's sixty-fifth birthday party at some snazzy Italian joint called Francesca's.

Benny didn't understand why her boss would invite his underlings to his own birthday party outside of work when he spent all his time already with them, but Benny didn't question it. It made Nesrine happy. He was grateful for the free dinner too. "Tell him okay," Benny said.

There weren't a lot of people in the gym at this hour, so it would work out in his favor. But he wouldn't feel good about the lack of work today.

The plumber arrived thirty minutes later. Bent under Benny's sink, the plumber asked, "Who fucked this up?"

"What does it matter?" Benny answered.

"I mean, it looks like someone watched a YouTube video or something and tried to fix it himself," the plumber said. "The drain line is all messed up. I need to replace the whole thing."

"The fuck out of here you do," Benny argued.

The plumber gave Benny an estimate, and Benny said, "I'm gonna call someone else," and the plumber left. It was noon and Keith was eating a meatball Parm hero from Lorenzo's Pizza. Benny felt a little better. Not because his fighter was eating—that was a given; he was light—but because Keith had chosen to go to Lorenzo's Pizza instead of Frank's Italian Ristorante. Lorenzo's Pizza was a slice shop. Three small tables and that was it. Frank's Italian Ristorante was a restaurant that served all the items of a slice shop but with the added luxury of a dining room and an extended menu. Its food was comparable to Lorenzo's, but the added dining area annoyed Benny, so he preferred Lorenzo's. It also had a better meatball Parm.

"Finish that up, kid. I need to get out of here early today."

Keith soaked up the last of the sandwich's sauce with the last of its bread and scooped up the last of its cheese and put it in his mouth. "Ready, Coach."

They worked punches to the body. "A good boxer has to be a good body puncher," Benny always told his fighters. "Hurt the body, and you'll hurt his head in ways he won't know why." The work was good and left Benny a little sore, but that soreness meant he was alive and not in the ground. A good reminder to smile.

Benny wore a black button-down dress shirt and his favorite blue jeans and the brown shoes that Nesrine liked to her boss's birthday party. The colors were mismatched, but the free food on his plate wasn't. He loved a free dinner. Felt like the holidays. He loved to see Nesrine happy too. And Nesrine was happy around her coworkers. Was happy that Benny never put up a fuss when these sorts of events sprang up. Not that he hadn't in the past, but as the years wore on, he had given up being cantankerous around them and just went with the flow. Nesrine also liked a free dinner.

Benny's wife had worked with the same people for years, so all small talk had already been talked at previous Christmas parties and other functions. They all knew he owned Hudson Boxing Gym, knew he was from Jersey City too. Knew he liked the Jets over the Giants and the Mets over the Yankees, and told the same lie they all told about how they would "never retire to Florida!" Knew he loved Nesrine and that they had no kids. Knew what they needed to know of him.

"Thank you," Nesrine said, and touched her husband's hand as they sat eating cake and drinking weak coffee at the end of the party.

This was a good night, Benny thought.

He met Keith at the Empress Diner the next morning.

"Looking beefy, kid," the trainer said to his fighter.

"I better be. Ate a whole pound cake before I went to sleep last night."

"Buster Davis eats pound cake in his sleep."

The logistics for Keith's heavyweight debut had been finalized weeks ago but were beginning to be discussed only now. The fight was taking place in the Newark Veterans Memorial Coliseum, a five-thousand-seat multi-use facility in the worst neighborhood of one of the worst cities in America. Keith was fighting on the undercard of the WBO Welterweight Championship. His fight would be the second of seven. No one in the audience was going to know a whole lot about him. Some might have seen him fight at cruiserweight in some ratty gym or casino before, but this would be Keith's first professional fight, in a professional arena, in front of professional judges, with a professional referee. It would have been hard to call Keith a professional before this fight because he'd only "fought bums, with bum refs," according to his trainer, so this fight would be a test of new nerves for the young fighter.

Benny scanned the diner for a waitress. "I want you at 210 pounds at least, kid. Buster's gonna be bigger than you no matter what, but maybe we can use some of your quickness to our advantage."

"Float like a wasp, sting like a butterfly," Keith said.

"That couldn't be any more wrong if you tried," Benny responded.

"I think me coming in lighter is gonna help, Coach. Did you see the video Buster Davis posted last night?"

"No, kid. I saw four minutes of *Jeopardy!* and then I went to bed."

"Maybe it was just me, but he looked kinda slow working the mitts."

"Listen, kid. Buster Davis isn't some chump. You can still back out of this fight."

"Coach! What are you talking about? The fight is in six days. I can't back out now. And why would I? I'm gonna win!"

"Say you broke your foot or something. There's always an excuse, kid."

And just as those words left Benny's mouth, he regretted them. He regretted them because he understood how they sounded to Keith Way. He understood how he sounded to Nesrine and Paulie. He understood a lot in a moment that he would soon forget. He wanted to bottle up the feeling, put it on a shelf, and take a swig from it whenever he needed to remind himself. He also wanted Keith to put more syrup on his French toast.

"Easy work, Coach," Keith said.

"Nothing's easy if it's work, kid," Benny said.

"Will that be all for you gentlemen today?" the waitress asked.

Benny paid the bill with his new Chase Rewards credit card. He signed up for it so he could take advantage of all the expenses that came with owning a gym. He was hoping to use the miles he earned to pay for his and Nesrine's next trip down to Florida.

The trainer and his fighter drove to the gym in silence. Not because there was nothing to be said, but because they simply didn't feel like talking. And that suited Benny fine. The traffic was light, which allowed the Cadillac to drive like it was supposed to. Free of interference and yield signs, they drove past Lorenzo's Pizza and the public library, Naggiano's Bakery and Temple Beth-El and William L. Dickinson High School. They drove through Jersey City like Jersey City wasn't there. They drove like the world wasn't there. They drove the way you would drive if you actually wanted to drive. They drove free of hassle all the way to the gym. Then they arrived. Then Benny noticed another Cadillac parked in his spot. A Cadillac belonging to a man Benny had hoped wouldn't come around so soon.

"How you doin'?" Mario "Skinny Legs" Rattazzi asked Benny as he walked inside Hudson Boxing Gym.

Fuck, Benny said to himself when he saw Mario sitting on the bench in front of the gym's front desk.

Mario "Skinny Legs" Rattazzi and Benny Schultz went all the way back to the sixth grade, when the two became next-door neighbors and friends. Benny would go on to take his fights into the ring. Mario brought his fights out onto the street. Mario was an associate of the DeCavalcante crime family, but he wasn't a made man because his mother was Egyptian and he had never earned his button. He had been running around the streets and prison ever since he dropped out of high school at the age of sixteen. A bookie and loan shark early in his career, Mario had been sent to jail for thirteen years after being pinched on a wire for heading a prostitution ring in eastern Pennsylvania. Out of jail only a couple of years, he had picked up his old line-making ways and was at the gym to get a little gossip out of Benny and to collect his monthly payment.

"How's the kid looking?" Mario asked Benny as the two of them walked to his office.

Mario held an interest in the gym, not because of muscle, but because of desperation. When Benny and Paulie first tried to open the gym, they couldn't get a loan to save their lives. Paulie told Benny he was "cash poor," which really meant that his money was tied up in a small, depreciating fishing boat that had drained his finances. So, like any good Jersey boy from the block in those days, they approached the other bank in the neighborhood. Mario loaned them $100,000. But when Mario got pinched, Benny had no one to make the payments to anymore. So he stopped making payments for thirteen years, thinking nothing of it. Then Mario got out and bought a new Cadillac. Then Mario remembered some of the money he still had on the street. Then Mario started hanging around the gym more.

Benny handed Mario an envelope with $1,000 cash in it. "Kid's looking good."

"How the lines looking?" Mario asked as he thumbed through the envelope. He wore an ill-fitting suit and shoes two sizes too big. Mario was fat in the belly but got the nickname Skinny Legs because he had the limbs of a flamingo. Benny always called him Mario.

"No idea, Mario," Benny said.

Mario was asking Benny who he thought was gonna win the fight. Not because he cared, but because he was taking illegal bets on the whole card. Figured he could get a little juice out of Benny. "You always so friendly to your friends?" Mario asked as he stood up and put the envelope inside his jacket pocket for safe-keeping.

"Only to friends like you."

Mario headed for the door and Benny felt relieved.

Mario "Skinny Legs" Rattazzi had never killed anyone. *He's in the Mafia, but not really,* Benny thought whenever the guy came around. Still, friends like him were friends you never wanted, especially in northern New Jersey.

"Keith! Why aren't you sweating?" Benny screamed across the gym as he exited his office behind Mario. Mario made everyone in the gym nervous, and for good reason, but once he left, the violent hip-hop on the stereo unfolded again, and Benny undid his belt and poured his third cup of coffee for the morning. He knew he would have to shit soon. "Work, kid!" he continued as he got into the ring with Keith.

Shoes unlaced, Keith asked, "What did he want, Coach?"

"To drop me off cookies. What do you care, kid?"

"Dude scares me. Is he in the Mafia? I didn't think they were still around."

"Who do you think owns the garbage companies, construction companies, unions, and politicians around here, kid? Tony Soprano? Life ain't a TV show. Enough questions! Let's get to work."

They worked hard that day—harder than they had worked in all of training camp. This was because Keith knew that his fight was getting closer and the extra hard work would help calm the new nerves in his belly. He never got nervous before his fights only because he felt that he would always win. And he had. But then he made the decision to move up weight classes. Keith knew Buster Davis would be his hardest opponent yet. Bigger, stronger, and with more Instagram followers. But Keith also knew that Buster Davis dropped his shoulders before he jabbed and that he tended to throw a 1-1-2-1 combo when setting up for a sweeping right hook. *Benny would know this too if he had an Instagram account,* he thought.

Keith Way knew all this because he followed only boxers on Instagram. And Buster Davis posted some of his favorite content. He also had 229,481 followers. But Keith wasn't counting.

———

Benny was having dinner tonight with Nesrine, Paulie, and Sherla at Golden Leaf Thai in Cliffside Park. Benny hated Thai food, and Nesrine knew this, so did Paulie, but it was Sherla's turn this time to pick the restaurant, and therefore Benny had no say in the matter. Once a month, these two couples went out to dinner with each other. To make it fun, they would take turns choosing which restaurant to go to. Last month was Nesrine's turn, and they had gone to Luccina's, an upscale Italian place in Bayonne. The month before that was Paulie's turn, and he had chosen a Mediterranean joint that was on Ninety-Second Street and Second Avenue in Manhattan called Palshmyra that they all enjoyed.

Month before that was Benny's turn. They went to the Empress Diner.

"Just get the chicken pad thai and some rice," Nesrine whispered into Benny's ear as the couples perused their menus. And like always, Benny did exactly what his wife said. He could trust Nesrine with menu choices as easily as he could trust her with his life. Life with her was easy. Life inside the ring wasn't.

"Gotta admit," Paulie said with a mouthful of khao soi, "the kid's looking good."

"Good for a cruiserweight," Benny said. "But not for a heavyweight. Don't know what the kid's thinking."

"Saw Mario couple of days ago," Paulie said.

"I saw him this morning," Benny said.

The wives knew Mario "Skinny Legs" Rattazzi. Knew him in the ways they wanted to know him. Knew that he had helped their husbands open their gym. Knew what they needed to know.

"Honey?" Sherla said to her husband. "Are you going to tell them?"

"Oh yeah. Almost forgot. Melissa got into Kellogg."

"Oh my god! Congratulations!" Nesrine beamed.

"Kellogg?" Benny asked. "She's gonna make Frosted Flakes?"

"Graduate school," Paulie corrected his oldest friend in the world.

"You must be so proud!" Nesrine said.

"Gonna cost me an arm and a leg," Paulie complained.

"Oh, stop it." Sherla slapped her husband's thigh.

Paulie had done all right for himself. After graduating from Ramapo College, he went on to get a job for AIG. Same commute, same building, same desk. Great with his clients' money, but awful with his own. Bought a place too big for a family of three. ("And a fucking boat!" Benny screamed at Nesrine when he had heard the news.) The gym a secondary matter to him always, just as working Keith's corner as a cutman was, Paulie never did any of this for a dividend payment. He did it to play a role in his own movie, the movie he dreamed about on coffee breaks from his forty-third-floor office. Dreams meant to be lived by other people but dreamt of by him. What dreams were really made of.

"I'm so happy for those two," Nesrine said to her husband on the ride home. "What an accomplishment."

"Good kid, that Melissa. Always has been. Hard work pays off." And with this thought, Benny became excited. *Proof in the pudding.*

They had the windows rolled down and both their elbows out. Benny saw a sign for a Baskin-Robbins and pulled into the parking lot with no notice to Nesrine. She laughed. No way she could say no now. The couple ate their ice-cream cones on the hood of Benny's Cadillac like young lovers. They weren't young themselves, but their love felt that way. *Hard work paying off,* Benny thought.

———

On Tuesday Keith met Benny at the gym. It was going to be a cardio day. Nothing else. They would work a full workout that day, have a day off, and then cease all activity until the weigh-in and then, finally, fight night. Keith weighed 205 pounds when he stepped on the scale in front of Benny and Donny.

"That a boy!" the gym manager screamed.

"Not bad, kid," Benny said.

"Thanks, guys." Keith smiled.

Cardio to Benny meant skipping rope, running miles, and burpees. Benny thought like a fighter from a different time, because that's exactly what he was. Cardio to Keith was the videos he watched on YouTube of doped-up UFC fighters running up hills with sleds attached to their backs and doped-up cyclists competing in road races, and this really hot black girl he followed on Instagram who ran on a treadmill for an hour with the camera of her phone zoomed in on her ass the entire time. Keith thought like a fighter from a new time.

"I don't want you sweating too much this next session, kid," Benny said during their lunch at Chili's.

Keith had ordered the southwestern egg rolls,

boneless wings, classic nachos with beef, mushroom Jack chicken fajitas, a large Coke, and a "Paradise Pie" for dessert. "You see that photo Buster Davis posted this morning?"

"Will you fucking stop asking me that question, kid?"

The fighter handed the trainer his cell phone. "Look."

On the screen was Buster Davis standing next to Teddy Burns and a couple of other fighters who belonged to Matchbook Promotions. This was the promotional company that Buster Davis was signed with, and Teddy Burns was its highly publicized founder and chairman. "A ruthless motherfucker who'd cut your dick off and feed it to you," as once described by Benny, Teddy Burns made stars out of fighters. Buster Davis wasn't a star yet, but Teddy Burns could change that. He could do the same for Keith Way.

"That photo has 2,411 likes, and he posted it thirty-eight minutes ago. How crazy is that?"

"You know what's crazy, kid? What's crazy is that the guy on the screen of your phone probably weighs twenty-five pounds more than you right now. What did you order for dessert again?"

"Ain't nothing, Coach," the fighter assured his trainer.

The waitress dropped off dessert and the check at the same time. Benny coughed, and Keith put down his credit card. They worked hard the rest of that day, and Keith threw up twice, but what mattered most was that they were there. That they had shown up again. That they were putting in the work like Melissa had, like Nesrine had, like all the people Benny tried to surround himself had. *I like good work,* he'd say if you asked him. But no one had to.

———

Keith Way hadn't had a day off from training—a real day off—in over two weeks. His body needed it. His relationship needed it too. Keith was like all young kids in a bond too deep for their own understanding, and Sabrina was his everything. And Keith was Sabrina's something. The game of love in 2019 played out through posts, dating apps, and DMs. You wouldn't know it if you looked, but behind the smiles and cupcakes and love songs and restaurant reviews and all the other nonsense Keith Way blasted on social media about the love of his life, the opposite could be said for the focus of his desire.

But Sabrina loved Keith because he was different from the douche bags she normally dated. "He's a professional boxer!" she boasted to her parents. They went to his fifth fight against Raymond Rael, held in the gymnasium of SUNY Cobleskill.

"I thought professional boxers fought for big

crowds?" Sabrina's father asked at dinner after the fight.

"They do," Keith answered, "when they have a blue checkmark and over a hundred fifty thousand followers."

As a surprise to his girlfriend, and a chance for a short road trip, Keith had bought tickets for Sabrina's favorite band, Lipslide, at the Stone Pony. The drive down was adventurous in the ways a drive down the Garden State Parkway in the summer can be: smelly and torturous.

"I haven't been here since I was a kid!" Keith announced as they arrived in Asbury Park. He parked the car on the street and bought a couple of water bottles. They drank them quick because the club wouldn't let outside beverages in. *Hope I'm not sweating too much,* Keith thought.

The show sucked: way too loud and the band wasn't very good. Keith didn't mind, though, because he got to be with Sabrina, and besides fighting, not much made him happier. When they got back to Keith's place that night, they curled up in bed and put on an episode of *Curb Your Enthusiasm* on the HBO account of Sabrina's cousin. Before Keith could tell his girlfriend she had to leave, Sabrina placed her hand on his penis. Keith attained an erection soon after.

"I can't, babe," he whispered.

"I don't care," she whispered.

The next morning, Keith was shadowboxing when

Benny walked in. *Something's off,* he said to himself about his fighter. *He seems too relaxed. Too laid-back.*

"You're sweating too much, kid," the trainer barked.

"Feeling good, Coach," Keith said. "Weighed in at 207 today."

"That's good, kid. But you know Buster Davis is gonna have the weight advantage. Don't be slippin' now."

Donny came over to the two of them. "Found a new video on YouTube that could help with your sink, Benny. Some dude on Twitter said that your plumber was an idiot too."

"Donny?" Keith asked. "How many followers does Buster Davis have on Twitter?"

"I'm surrounded by fucking idiots," Benny cried.

"Ninety-four K," Donny answered.

"Get out of here!" Benny screamed.

The trainer and the fighter watched tape and broke down game plans that day. Paulie stopped by to check on the cut that Keith and Benny still denied existed or had ever happened. Ideas were discussed. A couple more plumbing videos were played on the front desk computer. Seventeen Chips Ahoy! cookies were eaten with 2 percent milk and a side of garlic fries. The trainer and the fighter were as prepared as they were going to be for Keith Way's heavyweight debut on the undercard of Sanchez vs. Herschel at the Newark Veterans Memorial Coliseum in two more days. Everyone went home that night feeling good. Benny would pick up Keith tomorrow for the press confer-ence and weigh-in. *Nothing more to be done,* Benny said to himself as he got into the Cadillac. *Up to the kid now.*

———

The Cadillac had driven well. "Gotta eat more, kid," Benny said.

"I weighed 208.2 pounds this morning. I'm good, Coach," Keith said.

"Nonsense! What's the matter with you, kid?"

Keith's phone buzzed on the table at the Empress Diner. He got excited thinking it was a new notification on the photo he posted of himself standing on the scale this morning at 5:46 A.M. and showing the digital readout of his weight: *208.2.* But it wasn't. It was a text message from Sabrina.

"Still at the Empress?"

"Cool if Sabrina meets us here?" Keith asked his trainer.

Benny knew Sabrina would now be attached to his fighter's hip from here until the fight. Benny knew that a good fighter needed a good woman, but he was worried because Keith was an average fighter and Sabrina was far from good. Not that Benny was one to judge, but he could sense a darkness in the young partner of his fighter. *She's got the devil in her,* he'd say if Keith had asked him. But Keith Way was twenty-four years old and Benny Schultz was sixty-one. Keith looked to Benny for love advice in the way Benny looked to Keith for advice in anything. They didn't.

"Can I say no?" Benny asked.

Sabrina arrived at the Empress Diner eleven minutes later. In that stretch of time, Keith showed Benny the Facebook post that Buster Davis had made the previous night—*Can't wait to fite for all my homies Tmrw Night! Don't forget to buy a ticket or tune-in early. Thanx to Mr. Burns and all the peeps at Matchbook Promotions for giving me another EZ win and another step closer to my dream of the Belt!!"*—and also a video on YouTube of a missing Indonesian woman's dead body being cut out of an anaconda fully intact.

Sabrina smelled like the makeup department of Nordstrom. That is to say that Sabrina smelled like three thousand bottles of different perfume poured out into one giant bucket. She stunk up the diner. She stunk up their booth. She stunk up Benny.

"Hey, babe," she said to her boyfriend with gum in her mouth, and then took the gum out and stuck it under the table.

"Hey, smooches," Keith said, and rubbed his nose against hers.

Benny almost puked. "So, kid, after the weigh-ins, I don't want you two having any funny business, okay?"

What Benny didn't know was that Keith and Sabrina had fucked for close to three hours two nights before and then Keith had ordered three pizzas from Pizza Hut, and that was why he came in heavy on the scales the next morning and looked so loose shadow-boxing when Benny arrived at the gym.

Sabrina shifted in her seat.

"Of course, Coach," Keith said.

Benny didn't believe any of it.

"You nervous, honey?" Sabrina asked her boyfriend.

"He should be," Benny said.

"I'm ready, babe," Keith said. "Benny and I have worked hard. I got this."

"There's gonna be a lot of people there too, right?" Sabrina asked.

"There ain't gonna be no one there!" Benny barked. "He's the second fight on the undercard. Sun's still gonna be out when this kid's fighting."

They ordered pancakes, eggs, bacon, orange juice, coffee, bagels, Taylor ham sandwiches, and lox, and they split the bill three ways.

The weigh-ins for the fight were at the venue and soon, because Keith Way was fighting on the under-card, and Benny wanted to be there on time. Keith drove there with Sabrina in her car and Benny drove the Cadillac alone. He punched "Newark Veterans Memorial Coliseum" into Apple's Maps app and it gave him the options "Newark Veterinary Hospital," "Veterans Memorial Park," and "Veterans of Foreign War," but it didn't give him "Newark Veterans Memorial Coliseum." Even Benny knew Maps sucked, but it was on his home screen, and he kept using it and complaining about it for some reason rather than moving the icons on his phone so that Google Maps, which he preferred, was in place of Maps. *Fucking Apple Maps,* he said to himself.

"See the tits on that, kid?" Benny asked Keith as they made their way through the dressing room of the Newark Veterans Memorial Coliseum, a small arena that used to play host to the Newark Fury, the city's AAA hockey team from 1978 to 1996, but now accommodated circuses, college graduations, and the occasional concert. A drain on the resources and real estate of a city that could afford little of either, plans were in the works to tear down the arena and replace it with a multi-use retail/condominium space and a new drug rehab facility called Second Waves.

The dressing room was filled with winners and losers. *Mostly losers,* Benny thought. Gerry McConnell was also there.

Fuck, Benny said to himself as both gym owners met.

"Why're you here?" Benny asked.

"Good to see you too. How's the kid's tits looking?"

Keith was eating an everything bagel with cream cheese behind them.

"Tits are looking all right," Benny answered. "But man, some of the kids in this place. Unbelievable."

"Youth." Gerry slapped Benny on the back hard enough to remind him that their youth was far beyond them now. "It's a beautiful thing."

Benny looked at Gerry and became lost in thought. He became lost among the people in the room. He was lost because he wasn't at the gym, he wasn't at the Empress Diner, he wasn't with Nesrine. For a man like Benny, existence took place in a limited number of places. Limited numbers led to direct reasonings, and that led to discipline, which led itself to a routine that produced a reassurance that everything would always be predictable. He always got this way before a fight. Benny could assure himself in the fighters in his gym because they breathed the same air as him. He could assure himself in the fighters in the other gyms around northern New Jersey because they, unfortunately, breathed the same air as well. But these were different kids from different places. And different kids from different places who breathed different air led to different consequences. No one knew that better than Benny. *No one knows consequence more than me,* he'd say if people brought it up, but thankfully they never did. So he stewed with an anticipation of the unknown in a dressing room surrounded by his peers. Surrounded by the people stewing with the same anticipation as him, although Benny wouldn't have agreed. Death and taxes, potholes and cracked cell phone screens, Benny liked the guarantees in life. A fight was never guaranteed. Boxing was never guaranteed. Winning was never guaranteed. *But failure always is,* Benny thought. If only everyone knew what Benny knew.

"But seriously, why are you here?" Benny asked again.

"You think I was gonna miss this? The fuck else am I gonna do anyways? Sanchez vs. Herschel in my own backyard. Pulled all the strings I got to get back here."

"How you doing, Mr. McConnell?" Keith asked.

"How goes it, kid? Tits are looking good."

"Thanks," Keith said. "Excited for the weigh-ins?"

"Who the fuck's excited for a weigh-in?" Benny snapped. Surrounded by all these fighters and trainers and testosterone, Benny didn't feel bad about snapping at Keith. *Dumb question,* he thought.

"You guys gotta check this out." Keith held out his phone for the two old trainers to see.

On his Instagram feed was a livestream of Buster Davis pulling up to the Newark Veterans Memorial Coliseum. In the video stream, the fighter parked his Porsche and told his audience that he was "in the best shape of my life and gonna put this no-name to shame," and then walked through the same security door that Keith and Benny had walked through, and then strolled into the locker room that Keith, Benny, and Gerry were standing in now. Although Buster Davis was in the same room as them, all three continued to watch his live Instagram feed on Keith's iPhone instead of watching him film himself in person right in front of them. Then Buster Davis turned off his phone. He walked past his opponent and out to where the press and scales were. Keith put his iPhone back in his pocket.

"Kid's got great tits," Benny said.

That night, Benny and Nesrine went to Nesrine's favorite restaurant, Alfonso's, in Moonachie. The place had arguably the best osso buco and veal scaloppine in Bergen County, but they also went there because the husband of one of the women whom Nesrine worked with owned it. It had turned into a tradition to dine at Alfonso's the night before one of Keith's fight for Benny and Nesrine. The tradition had started simply because Keith's first-ever professional fight was in Moonachie and had to be postponed until the following night after a water main in the middle school gymnasium where it was being held sprung a leak. They all went to Alfonso's following this debacle because Nesrine had said, "I think Gabriella's husband's restaurant is in Moonachie." They went, and ate, and laughed, and they enjoyed the night that had been presented to them. They enjoyed an evening that was supposed to be enjoyed for the failure that it had brought. It was the kind of failure that anyone should understand. Even Benny knew that much.

"What did Buster Davis weigh?" Nesrine asked her husband.

"227 pounds," Benny said with a mouthful of veal. "Almost twenty pounds more than Keith."

"So what? Probably fat anyways."

"Fat? You see the tits on that kid?"

"No, Benny. I haven't seen 'the tits on that kid.'"

The waiter brought over more bread and refilled their waters. Nesrine ordered another glass of Chianti. Benny smiled.

"You look lovely tonight by the way," the husband told his wife.

"Oh, stop it." She blushed. Her face turned the color of her wine.

Benny loved that he could still make his wife feel pretty, because she was pretty. She was the prettiest thing in all of New Jersey to him. *Maybe not the world. Some of those Korean girls . . .* Benny would think. But even so, laying his eyes on Nesrine never made them droopy or tired, sad or quiet. More than the ropes of the ring or the smell of his gym, Nesrine was what made him want to wake up and get out of bed in the morning, made him want to strive to be a better man every day, if not for himself, then for her. Benny had stopped living for himself a long time ago. He stopped living for the greediness and desires that plagued a failed fighter, stopped living for the empty materials and filled-up lies that plagued a man with too big an ego. He wanted to live for something better, something more fulfilling than prizefights. He wanted to live for Nesrine.

They left in a better mood than when they had arrived. Benny and Nesrine made love that night in the way that people of their age made love. Their love couldn't have been stronger, and good thing for Benny, as he would need it come the next day.

Benny's phone buzzed at 6:43 A.M. It was a text message from Keith Way: *"LETS GOOOOOO COACH!!! FIGHT DAY!!!"*

Benny farted, pulled the blanket off his body, and walked to the bathroom. He turned on the shower and relieved himself of urine and any other leftover fluids down the drain of the shower as he stood outside it, waiting for the water to warm. The steam in the little room built quickly, and Benny waited for all his piss to clear from the tub's floor before stepping inside. The water tore through him like bullets, like smooth shards of glass, cutting his pores and his mind into a million pieces. The droplets of water carried with them the weight of the day. Leaping around his skin like hundreds of boxers hot on their feet in the ring, the drops slipped and rolled through the hair he still had left onto his shoulders and down arms that were used to holding muscle but now held old skin. Continuing over a stomach that had once housed abs but had become a potbellied hump, the beads marched down his penis, around his testicles, down his thighs and calves, and finally onto the floor and into the drain. *Wonder where it all goes,* Benny thought. Not about the water, but about time. "Hopefully not down the same drain," he said out loud.

"What was that, honey?" Nesrine said from outside the bathroom's open door.

"Nothing."

The trainer picked up his fighter soon after, and they went to the Empress Diner for a small breakfast. Keith Way had made weight, so this morning's meal was a light fruit platter, some coffee, and a pumpkin bagel with lox. Benny's superstition led him to order a ham and onion omelet. He didn't particularly like ham or onion, but this was what he had eaten before his very first pro fight, and he had won that fight. Won the next eleven too. The ham and onion tasted different after that.

"Tits are looking good, kid. But who eats lox on a pumpkin bagel?"

Keith was caught off guard by the compliment. "Thanks, Coach. Tits are feeling good too! Did you see the—"

"Listen, kid. No more phone. No more distractions. Not for the rest of the day. Heavyweight fighting isn't about Instalame and Fuckbook and Twitter."

"Funny you got that one right."

"I'm being serious, kid. You're getting into the ring with a different kind of man who wants a different kind of thing than you do."

And right there, Benny knew what he had done. Right in that moment, Benny knew he had planted the seed of doubt into his own fighter's head whether his fighter knew it or not. Right then and there, Benny lost his own fight. Right then, Benny had failed. Again.

"What are you talking about? We both wanna be heavyweight champion, Coach! Who wouldn't?"

Benny paid the check and drove his fighter in the Cadillac through weekender streets and onward to the Newark Veterans Memorial Coliseum. Benny let Keith do most of the talking on the ride over. Bits of the earlier conversation still stuck in his teeth; Benny flicked with his tongue the words he should have said. But none of that mattered now. There wasn't space for it. All that mattered was the fight, *because you're always gonna be fighting,* Benny said to himself. *All life is is a fight.*

The locker room buzzed with trainers, fighters, and press with their cameras. And everywhere Benny looked, every single one of these people was on their cell phone, tweeting and posting and sharing and retweeting and reposting and resharing and texting and messaging and viewing and scrolling and clicking and filtering and swiping and matching and saving and deleting and drafting and rearranging and downloading and reserving and shopping and reviewing and buying and investing and filming and emailing and analyzing and liking and commenting and listening and booking and doing anything else but that which had to do with fighting. Sadly, Benny was not surprised. What was there to be surprised about anymore? *This world is fucked,* Benny would have said if people asked him. And they would have all agreed.

The home team's locker room was being utilized

for media needs and the needs of the fighters in the main event of the evening. The visiting team's locker room was used to house all the other fighters and their trainers. One room, well over a dozen bodies, and lots of hand wraps.

Benny and Keith began their process.

Hand wrapping was a religion in boxing, and Benny prayed to its god daily. Fragile hands and wrists on a boxer were worse than a fat lip or low blow. The wrapping process was also crucial, as it provided the time for focus and one last excuse to sit down for the rest of the night.

His left hand hung over the back of a folding chair, Keith shook his right leg up and down in nervous anticipation, headphones in and listening to the band Phish. A buddy of his had taken him to one of their concerts at Madison Square Garden the previous year, and he was able to get a recording of the concert and had listened to it ad nauseam ever since. He liked the way the grooves made him feel and the way the guitar player with the funny last name played. He had loved the lights and the energy of the crowd. He would close his eyes in between songs and listen to the fans roar while pretending it was him they were roaring for. *Ladies and gentlemen, the heavyweight champion of the world, Keith Way!* He might have smoked a joint.

Paulie nudged Keith and took out one of his earbuds. "Look who it is, kid."

Lifting his eyes from his hands, Kenny took in the

sight of the AFC welterweight champion Rex Holiday. The AFC, or the American Fighters Championship, was a mixed martial arts organization that was popular between Maine and Florida and no farther west than Ohio. Ask someone in California and they'd be clueless. Ask anyone who was part of a legitimate gym on the East Coast, and the rumor mills started turning. Rumor was Keith Way had knocked out Rex Holiday in a sparring session when Rex was training for his AFC debut a couple of years back. But rumors were just that, right?

"Why's he here?" Keith asked his trainer and his cutman.

"Because he's royalty," they both answered.

It was true. On top of being the AFC welterweight champion, Rex Holiday was also from West Orange. The MMA world and the boxing world might have intermixed in both of these fighters' lifetimes, but their worlds would continue to remain as different as the police and fire department. Rex worked on his striking at Hudson Boxing Gym when he began his career, but once he won that first AFC fight, he took his business across the river, through the Jews in Williamsburg and into Canarsie and the infamous Flatland Boxing Club. Rumor was Keith Way had knocked out Rex Holiday in a sparring session when Rex was training for this very fight. But Benny didn't like rumors. He liked the truth. And he knew the truth.

"Don't worry about it, kid. How're your hands feeling?"

Benny always wrapped Keith's hands too tight, but Keith never said anything because no one ever said anything to Benny. "Feeling good, Coach!"

Buster Davis was on the opposite side of the room shadowboxing at the wall. He was sweating, and his tits looked beefy, and that had Benny worried for his fighter. But he wouldn't show that on his face. His fighter hardly knew Buster Davis was in the room, there were so many people in there. *Why reflect the worry?* He put Keith's white Winning boxing gloves over his wrapped hands and laced the gloves too tight. He would have tied them looser if Keith had ever said anything, but he never did, so Benny didn't. With his matching white trunks and their sponsored logos from O'Sullivan's Auto Parts in Fort Lee, Alfonso's in Moonachie, and Benny's very own Hudson Boxing Gym printed large on his ass, Keith looked like a fighter ready for his fight. *Just in the wrong weight class,* Benny thought.

The time had come for the first fight of the evening: a lightweight bout between two journeymen who couldn't hit a punching bag. That meant the fight might last its full scheduled length, and Keith Way would be waiting in the wings for his time to shine. Keith didn't mind waiting, but Benny couldn't stand it. For a man who liked to be everywhere early, he hated having to wait for anything. *Typical Jersey asshole,*

Benny thought of himself. And he was right. But he was a nice asshole. Only got angry when it was called for, which was often in this trainer's life. But not before a fight. "Never get angry before a fight," Benny preached. Anger led to confusion, and confusion in the ring was not what led to victory. "Save your anger for your concentration," Benny would say during training. "Be angry that you're concentrating so hard that you forget you're even concentrating!" That never made much sense to Keith, but he understood what his trainer was trying to tell him. He understood everything about Benny whether Benny knew it or not. Whether he knew it or not.

Sabrina popped her head into the dressing room. "Hey, baby! My mom and dad just got here. I'm going to go meet them in our seats."

"Big crowd out there, babe?" Keith asked optimistically.

"You could say that," his girlfriend responded.

Sabrina's cell phone buzzed with a notification from a dating app that Keith didn't know was downloaded onto her phone. If she had looked at her phone, she would know the message was from a Silvio from Paramus and read, *"Can still meet for a drink Monday night if you can?!"* and she would have pretended that it was a text from her parents. But not even she was so cruel as to bring such bad voodoo to her boyfriend before his first-ever professional fight at heavyweight. She would make sure to respond when she left. The girlfriend kissed her boyfriend and wished him luck. Keith watched her walk out the locker room. *I'm such a lucky guy,* he said to himself.

Benny, Keith, and Paulie continued to pay little attention to the crummy fighters who were gunking up the ring before the real fighters could show this crowd how a fight is supposed to be and bided their time backstage. A small TV on a stand was showing the live broadcast. No one watched it.

"How you doin', kid?" the trainer asked his fighter.

"Ready for victory, Coach!" the fighter promised his trainer.

I'm tired of failed promises.

The first fight finished halfway through the second round. Liver shot. KO. No one in the locker room had seen it. Worse yet, this quicker than anticipated finish now put the accelerator on the Keith Way vs. Buster Davis match, something neither the fighter nor his trainer had considered.

"I should post something, right?" the fighter asked the trainer.

"What the fuck's wrong with you, kid?!" the trainer rightfully screamed at his fighter. "You're about to step into the ring with a stone-cold killer, and you want to post a picture?!"

"Not a picture, Coach. I had a great idea for a Facebook post that could be really motivating for all the people tuning in."

"Shut up!"

"Way vs. Davis?" a production assistant called into the room. "Get ready; intros begin in ten minutes."

The realness of what was happening sucked the air out of Benny's lungs. *This is a bad idea,* he said to himself. *Should have never taken this fight. Coulda coasted out the cruiserweight division. Dumb fool.* But like a well-trained double agent, Benny's face never showed what his mind thought. The stories in his head were for him only, not for publication.

Keith Way started moving around in his hooded white robe. He looked like a professional boxer, but he didn't move like one. He moved like *a kid who doesn't know what he's getting himself into,* Benny was thinking as he, Paulie, and their fighter walked through the locker room and into the hallway that led out into the arena. The pictures of minor-league hockey and basketball players along the wall made Benny think they were in an amateur fight and not a professional bout. He prayed his fighter wasn't thinking the same, because if he was, then the fight was already lost. *Doubt it,* he thought. *Kid probably can't wait to post every dumb thought that comes through his head between rounds.*

Benny held the same thought about his fighter as he did with all other fighters, and that was because the kids of this generation truly scared Benny. Technology truly scared Benny. Change truly scared Benny. But fighting had never made Benny truly scared. *And these kids don't know shit about fighting,* Benny would have said if you asked him. But no one did, and now he was scared. Scared for his fighter and the weak mind he possessed and the even weaker chin. Benny was scared for his fighter to taste real defeat. *Tastes different than banana pancakes. Lot different,* he mused. Why Benny thought his fighter was going to lose he didn't know, but what he did know was to make sure his fighter left that fucking phone in the locker room.

The restlessness was reaching a tipping point when, before Benny could say, *Maybe we shouldn't do this,* Keith's intro music came over the PA system. "Eye of the Tiger." Benny could have puked. Keith's hood thrown over his head, gloves at his side, the fighter, the trainer, and the cutman walked out to the bright lights and dull sounds of the Newark Veterans Memorial Coliseum at 4:41 P.M. on a Saturday afternoon in the summer with no air-conditioning.

Keith Way didn't look at the thin crowd as he made his entrance to the ring. He did hear his girlfriend yell his name and scream, "Kick his fucking ass!" but not even that really registered. This fighter was as focused as a lion hunting its prey, a sniper locked on to a target, and his target would be Buster Davis. But Buster Davis was still backstage taking photos to post on Instagram, and the only thing Keith Way could focus on now was not tripping on his too-long robe. *That would definitely make the front page of r/boxing on Reddit,* he thought as he marched along the runway and up the steps leading into the ring. The ropes were red. A giant Budweiser logo plastered itself in the middle of the canvas. The referee was bald. The lights were hot. His wraps were too tight.

"Don't wear yourself out, kid," Benny spoke into his fighter's ear. "Gonna be a long fight."

Before Keith could give Benny a smart-ass response, the lights of the coliseum turned off. Not a power outage, as some might have thought, but the beginning of the grand entrance of Buster Davis. "Hot in Herre" by Nelly spun on the PA system. Green laser beams sliced through the audience. The fighter held his iPhone in his right glove and livestreamed his entrance to his 230,161 followers, parading down the runway, up the stairs, through the ropes, and into the middle of the ring, focusing his phone on the Budweiser logo before tossing the apparatus to one of his cornermen.

The moment had arrived. Buster Davis had arrived. Keith Way had arrived. Benny Schultz wanted to run.

The referee brought the two fighters into the middle of the ring. With a microphone shoved in front of his face, he explained the same rules he said were explained earlier in the dressing room but never were and told both fighters to go to their respective corners.

Benny put Keith's mouthpiece in. "Listen, kid. Ain't nothing new, just more weight. Work that jab this round. Learn his distance."

"Jab. Distance. Got it, Coach," Keith agreed.

The bell rung, the audience cheered, and the fighters marched toward each other.

Keith Way threw a jab and it fell short. It fell short because Buster Davis held the reach advantage. With a counter right, Buster graced Keith's chin. The sweet music it produced amplified in the fighter's brain.

"Jab and move!" Benny screamed. "Move, kid. Can't hit ya if he can't find ya!"

Keith listened; he moved, jabbed, and connected. His left hand felt like lead against Buster Davis's forehead. It felt like lead because Buster Davis's head was lead. The fighters moved against each other, and the ref soon broke them up. Buster threw a quick right hand in the melee. Collected and calm, Keith's left foot began to do his talking. Moving wide to the right of Buster Davis's taller body, he threw a hook that connected with the rib cage of his opponent. Keith heard him wince.

Benny hadn't dreamed it would go like this. He thought Buster would come charging in early and try to overpower his fighter with his weight and height. But Benny saw his flaw way before Keith would ever have seen it watching the tape after the fact. Benny could see that Buster tended to flinch with his right hand before he threw his jab. When he flinched, he threw. And when he threw, he was open. And if he was open, then Keith could get him. The bell rung and the first round was over.

"Good round, kid," the trainer told his fighter. Paulie poured water over his head.

"Strong guy," Keith said between gasped breaths.

"Listen, kid. Watch the right hand. Guy flinches the right hand when he's gonna throw the jab."

The crowd was louder than its size showed. Keith was having trouble hearing Benny with the ringing in his head. "Right hand. Jab. Got it," he replied.

The bell rung and the fighters met once again in the middle of the ring.

Keith Way went on the attack. Bending down, digging in, he threw Benny's logic out the window like a cigarette and decided he was going to need to work the body and wear this larger fighter down instead. Taking hooks to the torso, Buster answered back with hooks to Keith's head. The shots were hard, but so were Keith's. It was boxing the way fans always wanted to envision it. It was exciting and dangerous. It held rules all its own. It was real. They broke away from each other, and Buster threw his jab. And before he threw his jab, he flinched his right hand. But Keith didn't see it, because he chose not to see it. He chose to let the animal instincts of his mind overtake the human rationalities he had trained weeks to remember and then forget. He remembered the forgetting part but had forgotten the remembering part. He was a fighter. He was fighting. But the fighting was tough. The bell rung and the second round was over.

"What the fuck's the matter with you?!" Benny screamed. "You ever listen to anything I tell you?!"

"Sorry, Coach. Good round, though."

Paulie looked at Keith's eye as he compressed his

cheeks with his enswell. He could see the old cut working new magic. "Keep an eye on that eye, kid," he told Keith.

"The jab, kid!" Benny barked. "Keep an eye on that jab!"

The bell rung and the fighters met once again in the middle of the ring.

Keith Way knew the cut on his eye would open in this round. He knew because it should have opened in the last round but hadn't because he had felt it coming and buried his face into Buster Davis's body to avoid any further damage to it. He had a feeling the judges had scored that round in his favor, though. The first round had gone to Buster Davis. This round started the same way the last ended. With brutality.

The heavy hands of Buster Davis made their way across Keith Way's body and head. Keith threw back, but he was throwing at air. He hit the air with force. Buster Davis countered with more force. The explosion was quick. The blood on his face was quicker. The cut was big but not too big. The blood tasted like pancakes. He moved out of Buster Davis's reach and his back hit the ropes. He hit the ropes because he was in a boxing ring, in a boxing match, with a heavy-weight boxer. There was nowhere else for him to go. He heard Benny yell, "Fight, kid!" Pawing at the blood that was congealing in the corner of his eye, he pinched his elbows tight to evade the punches that were landing with precision and looked up at the clock. *Fifty-eight more seconds.* He threw a right that got blocked. He threw a low left hook that landed. He threw with everything he had, and it felt like he was throwing nothing at all. It felt like he was fighting with air. And the air was winning.

The bell rung and the third round was over.

"Fuck," Paulie said, doing whatever he could to help the half-inch cut on Keith's eye.

"Work it, Paulie!" Benny screamed. "Listen, kid. I'm telling you what ya don't want to hear, so maybe that's why you ain't listening. But that reach is killing you. Need to look for his tells, kid!"

Paulie worked and Benny yelled, and the bell rang and Keith stood up and the fighters met once again in the middle of the ring.

The blood poured after the third jab.

Not how this was supposed to end, Keith Way thought.

"Not how I thought this would end!" Benny yelled at Paulie.

The fighters fought and the announcers announced. The crowd cheered and the trainers screamed. But Keith Way heard none of. He saw none of it. He felt none of it. All he was aware of was the power and size that was Buster Davis, the followers and the posts and the likes just as strong as his dips and punches and feints. Keith Way was lost in a daze of all that could have been. He was lost between the ropes he thought he knew so well. He was lost and . . .

2

———

The trainer and his fighter sat across from each other at the Empress Diner on a Monday morning in mid-September. It had been almost a month since Keith Way's loss in the fourth round by KO to Buster Davis at the Newark Veterans Memorial Coliseum in the second fight on the undercard of Sanchez vs. Herschel. The time had moved like gravy to Benny but like butter to Keith. The age of innocence lost in both; but the age of time was still much different between them. Benny felt the future like a man stubbing his toe in the dark. Keith felt the future like a man getting a blow job in the morning. Still, today what they both felt was failure. Their definitions were only slightly different.

"Cut's looking good, kid," Benny said.

"Thanks," Keith replied.

They didn't say anything else for a little while.

Keith was eating two eggs with whole wheat toast and a fruit platter. Benny was eating pancakes with hash browns and a buttered corn muffin. They were both eating their words.

"Listen, kid. Might make sense to take some time off and reassess your next move. I was thi—"

"I'm retiring, Coach."

"What?"

"Yeah."

"What?"

Benny never thought Keith would quit, because Keith Way wasn't a quitter like Benny Schultz was. Surely he hadn't taught his own faults to this fighter. Surely he hadn't spearheaded a campaign to take him down into the hole of ruin he put himself into on the daily.

Before Keith could answer, Benny's phone buzzed. It was a text from Nesrine. *"Don't forget dinner tonight!"* Benny would have known what it read had he looked at it, but he didn't. He knew who it was, and he knew what it said. They were eating with Paulie and Sherla at La Cantina in East Rutherford. Benny was happy he had remembered, because it meant his ship hadn't sailed yet. His emotions and his thoughts were still anchored down in a harbor somewhere in the Hudson River outside the windows of his gym. Next to the dead bodies and deader souls, his ship was steady. Its captain wasn't.

"We can just move back down to cruiserweight,"

Benny said, working hard to begin the worst kind of argument: an argument with someone who didn't want to argue.

"Nah, Coach."

The sparkle had perished. Benny saw it when Keith's head smacked against the canvas. The referee barely got to three in the count before waving his hands above his head and calling off the fight. Keith was unconscious for close to ten seconds, but if you had asked him, he would have told you it felt like nothing. And that's what he told the reporters and his fans on social media. That's what he told Sabrina and her family. That's what he told everyone at the gym and at Lorenzo's. That's what he told himself in the mirror the next day. But that's not what his eyes told Benny. His eyes told Benny that old story of big ideas and big wins that had met their ends. The finish line to a race they hadn't known they were running. Fighting for breath and fighting for significance in a world missing the need for them, Keith Way had decided enough was enough.

"I'm gonna go back to school, finish up my degree," Keith Way explained to his ex-trainer. "This fight game, it ain't what I signed up for, Coach."

"What's that mean?"

"It used to be the work and the progress that got me going. Somewhere, I don't know where, that all turned into whoring myself out for the good of no one but my own hidden ego."

"You're losing me, kid."

"This!" Keith held up his iPhone. "It turned into this. Boxing turned into this. Life somehow turned into this. It all turned into this."

Benny took another bite of pancake and nodded his head in a way that signified he understood what Keith was saying. In truth, he had no fucking clue what the kid was talking about. "I'm not gonna say it's the wrong choice, kid. It's a brutal sport. Tits looked great in that fight."

Keith laughed. "You're not angry?" he asked.

Benny was angry. He was sad, he was happy, he was relieved, he was disappointed, he felt scorned, and he understood. He understood what this young man was trying to tell him. This young man who he had once been, rolling around inside a world of his own making. *The ring gets smaller the more time you spend inside it,* he wanted to tell Keith. *The ropes looser and the punches harder.* But Keith didn't need to hear that because Keith knew that now. Benny wouldn't waste his breath.

"I can't be, kid," he answered. "To be angry at you would be to be angry at myself."

Keith nodded his head in a way that signified he understood what Benny was saying. In truth, he had no fucking clue what his ex-trainer was talking about. "I'll still be at the gym," he said.

No, you won't, Benny said in his head. "Of course you will, kid."

They split the check and walked outside together.

The morning was hot enough to make you pack up your belongings, leave your family, and drive straight to the North Pole. It was hot enough you'd rather be dead.

"Need a ride?" the ex-trainer asked his ex-fighter.

"Nah. Sabrina is gonna meet me here. We're going to the nursery to get some plants for the new place."

"I'll see ya around, kid."

"I'll see ya around, Coach."

Benny got in the Cadillac and turned on the engine. It stalled for a second longer than normal. So did Benny when he said through the open window, "Hey, kid. I'm not your coach anymore." It was said in the way good friends with a grudge spoke. People who would connect again in ways they weren't sure how, because that was life. That was boxing.

Keith Way, former professional cruiserweight boxer who had once dreamed of being the heavyweight champion of the world, chuckled in the way good friends who used to have a grudge chuckled. "Drive safe."

Benny drove to the gym. It was crowded. There was a boot camp class being taught by their newest employee, Geena, and Juan was hosting a small class of ten students on footwork. The buzz of the gym brought about a buzz in Benny as he sat down behind his desk and thumbed through the envelope Mario would be picking up from him soon enough. With a full envelope and an empty agenda, Benny, for the first time in he couldn't remember, felt lost. His phone rang. It was Nesrine.

"What's wrong? Where are you?" she blurted out into his ear.

"What are you talking about? I'm at the gym."

"I texted you. You didn't text me back."

Shit. "Sorry. Long story. Dinner tonight."

"I'm going to have to meet everyone there. My hair appointment got bumped. Can you please wear the green polo shirt? I'll hang it up in the closet for you."

Her voice was the best thing he'd heard all day. "Anything you want."

He hung up and hung back in his chair. He stared at his poster of Benny Leonard. Paulie came in and talked with him about a potential purchaser for the gym, but Benny was having a hard time hearing him. He was having a hard time with the fresh news in his head. He gave Paulie the summary, and Paulie wasn't surprised. "Smart kid," Paulie said. "I'll see you at dinner."

Benny went home and put on the green polo shirt, black jeans, and black New Balance sneakers. Eating with Nesrine, Paulie, and Sherla at La Cantina in East Rutherford tonight would provide a treat to an unsavory day. Mexican food in New Jersey was always a toss-up, but La Cantina provided an authentic Mexican feel and had the cuisine to back it up. "They do good work in that kitchen," he'd say whenever they ate there and the conversation inevitably turned to the authentic recipes.

That evening, seated around a square table with a clean yellow-and-red tablecloth, the two couples talked about Keith.

"I can't blame him," Sherla said.

"Neither can I," agreed Nesrine. "He has too much potential for other things. And he's so young."

"As long as that eye heals up well, shouldn't affect his complexion," Paulie piped in.

Benny chewed on his chicken enchiladas and said nothing. He said nothing, because in his mind was a conversation running too fast for anyone at the table to keep up with.

Potential. That's why we're all at this table. Because of our potential. That's why the busboy is here. Because of his potential. And the hedge fund manager to our left. And the violinist to our right. It's potential that brings us all to the place where we are, the place where we belong. It's potential that leads men into battle. It's potential that gets us up out of bed and into another day. It's potential that blocks out the evil and plugs in the neutral to equal a dash of normal. It's potential that does all these things. But we never think about the potential of failure, because if we did, the potential of anything else would become irrelevant. The potential to fail would become too big to fail itself. Benny would have said all this out loud if he thought anybody in the restaurant wanted to hear it, but he knew they didn't. *Who would?*

With the trust of knowledge and the beginnings of change springing upon him, Benny closed his eyes and savored the taste of the corn tortilla and salty sauce on his palate. He savored the taste of a life lived and of lessons learned. Before he could speak out about how appreciative he was for the life he still was able to taste, his phone buzzed. From his pocket the rather large device came, and on its screen was an iMessage from Keith Way and a link to a video. Benny opened the link, which led to a video of Buster Davis working out. Keith Way wrote to him the one thing that Benny would always need to hear.

"Kid's got great tits."